The Bride of Osiris

The Bride of
OSIRIS

Otis Adelbert
Kline

First Fiction House Edition January 2018

isbn 978-1947964235

www.FictionHousePress.com

The Bride of Osiris

CHAPTER 1
THE POCK-MARKED MAN

"**A**LAN, that man has followed us here! Look!"

Alan Buell glanced guardedly in the direction indicated by the frightened blue eyes of his dancing partner. He saw two men seated at a table edging the dance floor. The one nearest him did not appear extraordinary — just a plain man-about-town, middle-aged and a bit portly — the kind one meets at every turn in Chicago's places of amusement. The other presented a striking figure. He was tall and broad-shouldered and sat with the erect carriage of a soldier. A black, square-cut beard hid the lower part of his features, accentuating the prominence of his aquiline nose, above which his heavy eyebrows met in a straight line. In his piercing black eyes as they swept the room was the look of one accustomed to command.

Alan's eyes returned to those of his troubled fiancée as the intervening dancers shut the black-bearded man from view, and he smiled slightly.

"I don't know that we can do anything about it,

Doris," he said. "This is a free country, you know, and we're in a public café."

Doris Lee pouted prettily.

"I wish you would be serious for just one minute, Alan. You know that man has stared at me across the orchestra pit all season. I haven't been able to enjoy the opera one bit on account of him. Now he grows bolder and follows us to this café. Of course he hasn't done anything one could openly resent, but I've noticed his covert glances time and again, and I'm afraid."

"Perhaps," replied Alan, dryly, "he thought you were staring at him and was trying to confirm his suspicions."

"Alan Buell, you are exasperating tonight. If you could only realize how I feel. Why, I fairly shudder every time we pass that table."

When they passed the black-bearded man again Alan looked at him with unconcealed ire. He was lazily lighting a long Oriental cigarette, the while he attended the animated conversation of his companion.

The music stopped with a raucous syncopated wail and they returned to their table.

"If that man makes you nervous let's go somewhere else," suggested Alan.

He summoned the waiter and asked for the check.

"I don't believe I care to dance any more. My

nerves are in shreds. Take me home, please."

As they made their way between the tables many admiring glances were cast on Doris by the late diners. Alan noticed them, and although he had always been proud of her sparkling beauty, somehow he resented the attentions paid her at the moment. He looked sharply at the black-bearded man, but that individual still appeared absorbed in the conversation of his pudgy companion.

Pausing to don his topcoat at the check stand while Doris walked slowly ahead, Alan suddenly heard a scream of terror. He ran forward, hatless, an awful fear gripping his heart. The doorman, resplendent in blue and gold braid, lay on the floor, blood trickling from a gash in his temple. Beyond him two men were dragging Doris, kicking, struggling and screaming, into a waiting car!

Alan reached the running board with a frantic leap, just as the car started. He wrenched at the handle of the rear door but found it locked. A brutal, pock-marked face glared out at him. Beyond that face he saw Doris still struggling with the second man. In desperation he smashed the glass with his bare fist, and reaching within, grappled with the man with the pock-marked face.

The second abductor, seeing his companion in danger, suddenly whipped a blackjack from his pocket and brought it into play. At the first blow Alan hung on doggedly, but at the second he toppled from the now rapidly moving car, rolled over and over, and struck the curbing with a crash. Then came oblivion.

CHAPTER 2
THE MYSTIC SYMBOL

WHEN Alan Buell regained consciousness he was propped against the curbing, supported by two men. One was short and rotund of body, with a pink, babylike face. The other was a huge, burly individual with a bristling, iron-gray mustache and a half-concealed twinkle about his eyes that belied the frowning brow.

"Feeling better, boy?" he asked.

"I feel all right," responded Alan, weakly attempting to rise. "Where's Doris?"

"Whoa! Not so fast, lad, not so fast," said the big man, restraining him. "Rest for a minute or two. Then we'll let the doctor decide whether you leave in an ambulance or a taxi."

"Is Doris safe?" he asked, still struggling to get up.

"Don't know yet," replied the big man, and there was a note of kindness in his voice despite its gruffness. "Four flivver squads are chasing the kidnapers, and the police all over the city are on the lookout for them. They ought to run them down soon."

A coupé stopped near them with shrieking brakes, and a slender, gray-haired man carrying a surgical case stepped out.

"You made good time, Doc," boomed the big man.

"Not so bad, Chief," was the reply. He stopped beside Alan and examined him with deft, exploring fingers.

"No broken bones, only a few bruises and scratches," he announced. "The left hand seems badly lacerated."

For the first time Alan became conscious of the fact that his left hand pained him severely. The fingers were tightly clenched and ragged cuts smeared with half-dried blood showed on the knuckles.

"Looks as if you had been teasing a wildcat," said the surgeon, moistening some cotton with the fluid from a bottle taken from his case. "Relax those muscles, man. Give your blood a chance to work for you."

Alan opened his fingers stiffly. As he did so a small, glittering object fell from his grasp, clattering to the pavement.

With a grunt of surprize, the big man retrieved it, then examined it curiously while the doctor dressed the injured digits. Presently he handed it to his shorter companion.

The latter, as soon as he saw it, showed intense amazement.

"My God, Chief!" he exclaimed; "what is such a symbol doing here?"

"Know what it represents?"

"Not in modern society. It's like a voice from the tomb. I once studied—" He hesitated and looked significantly at Alan and the doctor. "Tell you about it later."

"All right." The big man took it from him, turned it a few times under the light, and dropped it in his vest pocket.

"Guess you've been holding out on us, lad," he said, when Alan, his hand swathed .in bandages, was assisted to his feet. "I think you had better come along over to headquarters."

"Who are you, anyhow?" asked Alan.

"I'm McGraw. This man is Hirsch, head of our fingerprint department. The man who dressed your wounds is Dr.. Brown."

Alan had read much of the activities of Chief of Detectives McGraw, and now recognized him as the subject of numerous photographs published in the newspapers when particularly striking exploits of his department had been brought to the public notice.

"Guess I should have recognized you before, Chief," said Alan, "but my head was sort of fuddled from the blackjack."

"Used a blackjack on you, did they?" said the chief good-naturedly. "Didn't know whether you got those bumps before you fell or when you lit."

"I wouldn't have fallen so easily without them."

"No, I guess you wouldn't, lad. Witnesses said you put up a pretty stiff fight, but they couldn't see the clouts you got in the cab. My car is parked down by the café. We'll get it and drive to headquarters."

The drive to headquarters, only four blocks distant, was a matter of minutes, but they seemed like hours to Alan, impatient for news of Doris. As he alighted from the car, his head still reeling from the blows of the kidnapers, it seemed that he was experiencing a hideous nightmare — that he must presently awaken to find it all a dream. When they reached the outer office the voice of the chief addressing a pale, slender young fellow industriously pounding the keys of a typewriter, recalled him to grim reality.

"Any news of the kidnaped girl, Jamison?" he inquired.

"Nothing yet, Chief."

"Come into my office and bring your notebook."

They followed the chief into the private office. He waved them to seats, unlocked his desk, raised the roll top and sat down heavily.. From a lower drawer he produced a box, and offered some thick black cigars to all in turn. Jamison politely refused and Hirsch took a cigar. Alan looked at the stalwart Havanas with some misgivings.

"Have a smoke," said the chief. "It'll quiet your nerves."

Somewhat in doubt about the effect on his nerves, Alan complied.

McGraw tucked a cigar far back in his cheek, lighted it, and leaned across the glass-topped table. Jamison rapidly thumbed the pages of his notebook, stopped, and held his pencil in readiness.

"Your name and address," said McGraw.

"Alan Buell, 18 Circle Court," he replied.

"You're not the son of Will Buell, the importer?"

"Will Buell is my father."

McGraw turned to Jamison.

"Put down 'Buell & Son, Importers, West Kinzie Street.' "

The chief toyed for a moment with the small glittering object that had dropped from Alan's hand.

"Who was the young lady with you?"

"Doris Lee, my fiancée, daughter of Professor Lee of Evanston."

"Where did you get this?" The chief leaned forward suddenly and thrust the glittering object under Alan's nose. It was a flat, square piece of beaten gold with a small ring, to which were attached a few links of chain. On one side a burnished convex disk stood out in relief. On the other was a raised figure of a throne surmounted by an eye.

Alan looked puzzled.

"I don't know," he replied. "I never saw the

thing before. What does it represent?"

"You know well enough what it represents or you wouldn't have tried to hide it from me."

"But I didn't try to hide it."

"What?" The chief scowled unbelievingly at him across the table.

"I think he's tellin' the truth, Chief," Hirsch cut in. "Looks to me like he tore it off one of the kidnapers in the fight and had a kind of death-grip on it when they knocked him out."

"Maybe you're right at that. It looked suspicious the way he clutched it and then dropped it on the pavement. There are so many secret societies these days a man doesn't know whom to trust."

"I can assure you that I don't belong to any of them," said Alan with some show of spirit.

"I believe you, lad, but you know it's the business of a detective to examine every possibility. I suggest that you jump in a taxi and go home now. We will notify Miss Lee's parents and do all we can to save her. You're not in shape to be of any help around here and a night's rest will do you good. I'll ring you up as soon as we get news of the girl."

CHAPTER 3
A CLUE AND A TRAP

THE next morning Chief McGraw, his after-breakfast cigar tucked snugly in his cheek, drove up before headquarters and was about to step out of his car when he saw something across the street that caused him to pause in astonishment. Then, quickly leaping out, he crossed to where a cab was parked near the curb. He peered inside and saw Alan Buell, still in evening clothes, his head bandages awry and those on his hand presenting a rather soiled appearance, curled up on the cushions, sound asleep. He addressed the driver, who was nodding drowsily over the wheel.

"Where the devil have you been all night?"

"If you'd ask me where we ain't been I could tell you better," replied the driver. "Are you a friend of dis guy?"

"I'm McGraw of the detective bureau."

"Holy cats! We didn't do nothin' but drive around, east, west, north and south. He slipped me fifty bucks and kept me goin' first one way, then another. At six bells this mornin' we're clear to the city limits on the north side and I asks him where to. He says come back here. When we get here he's poundin' his ear just like you see him, so I park the car and wait for him to wake up. He's still got about ten bucks worth of service comin'."

"All right. Let him sleep.. I suppose he'll want to see me when he wakes up. I'll be in the office until noon."

"I'll tell him, sir, when he wakes up."

An hour later McGraw looked up from the stack of reports on his desk as Jamison entered.

"Mr. Buell to see you, Chief."

"Show him in."

Alan Buell, still in disheveled evening clothes, entered and took the chair indicated by the chief. The latter anticipated the question on his lips before he could speak.

"Sorry, lad. We have no news of Miss Lee yet."

Alan's face fell and he sat for a moment in sorrowful silence. When at length he spoke, there was a glint in his eyes and a determined set to his jaw.

"Chief, I wonder if you would do me a special favor?"

"What favor, lad?"

"I'd like a job—and an assignment to this case."

McGraw removed his cigar from his cheek and stared at the youth in open-mouthed amazement.

"Why—er—I don't know. Most of the men on my force have done their turn in the harness before they were promoted to this work. But what about your father and your business?"

"That's all fixed up. I 'phoned Dad a few minutes ago and he told me to go to it if—if it would help to relieve my feelings. I don't care about the pay—would rather that you wouldn't pay me—but I've simply got to find Doris."

"Hum. Tell you what I'll do. I'll make you a special officer. You can consider yourself hired, and your first orders are to go home and clean up and rest up. Drop in after lunch and I'll start you off."

PROMPTLY at 1 o'clock Jamison ushered Buell into the office of the chief. McGraw looked up from a pile of reports he was scanning.

"Take a seat, lad," he said. "Send Rafferty in, Jamison."

Buell sat in silence while the chief shuffled the papers before him. Presently Rafferty came in. He was short, about five feet five inches, but powerfully built, with bulging neck muscles, broad shoulders and long, capable-looking arms. The scattered freckles on his merry Celtic countenance matched the copper hue of his hair and eyebrows. He walked with a rolling stride that suggested recent acquaintance with the deck of a ship. His age could not have been more than twenty-seven.

"Dan, this is Mr. Buell, the new man I told you about," said the chief. "Mr. Buell—Mr. Rafferty."

As the two men acknowledged the introduction, Buell noted the viselike grip of those strong fingers and reflected that Rafferty would be a mean antagonist in a rough-and-tumble.

"Jamison will sign you up and give you your badge and equipment," continued McGraw. "Rafferty has his orders and will show you the ropes from then on. Good luck to you, lads."

Some minutes later, with a badge pinned to his vest, an automatic resting snugly against his hip, and Dan Rafferty shuffling along beside him, Detective Alan Buell went to work on his first assignment. Rafferty had the curious gold ornament he had torn from the man with the pockmarked face, and a list of jewelry stores they were to visit.

"The chief says to show this to all the joolers an' try to find out where it was bought and by who," said Rafferty. "A moighty slow job he picked fer a couple av young bloods that craves excitement."

"You are fond of a fight, I take it." Buell noted the husky build of his companion.

"No more and no less than any thrue Irishman. Wrestlin' was me dish in the navy. I held the middleweight belt av me submarine squadron whin I was discharged. Me joints are gettin' rusty wid lack of exercise on this job."

"How long have you been on the force?"

"About six months this time, though I wore the harness a couple av years before I jined the navy, and divvil a bit of fightin' have I seen." There was a look of genuine regret in his blue eyes. "If we could only meet up wid them lubbers that ran off wid yer girl, now, it wouldn't be so bad."

"It wouldn't," agreed Buell heartily.

A thorough canvass of the loop jewelry stores, taking the rest of that day and all of the next, failed to yield a single clue. Three more days spent in calling on the outlying stores and pawn-shops were fully as discouraging.

The end of the third day—a rather strenuous one—found them in that part of the city on the south side known as the "Black Belt." They had just completed a thorough interrogation of an "Uncle" who loaned money on, bought and sold everything from the gaudy gewgaws so dear to the hearts of the neighborhood gentlemen of color down to second-hand underwear, and were making their way to the corner for the purpose of boarding a downtown street-car, when a large limousine backed slowly out of a garage, blocking the sidewalk for a moment.

Buell glanced casually at the limousine as it glided out before him, then looked again with a surprized gasp of recognition, as the driver shifted his gears and whirled away. Grabbing Rafferty by the arm he pointed excitedly in the direction of the departing automobile.

"Look!" he cried. "There's the kidnaper's car!"

"The divvil!"

Rafferty whisked pad and pencil from his pocket and took down the license number.

"We'll give the chief a ring," he said. "Are yez sure that's the right bus?"

"Positive. That's a specially built body. I don't believe there's another just like it in Chicago."

"Some millynaire's private gig, eh? We'll run him down aisy, now."

They entered the garage office and obtained permission to use the telephone. Rafferty called headquarters.

"Hello, Chief. This is Dan Rafferty. Buell just spotted the kidnapers' car." He referred to his pad, then gave the license number and description. "It's cruisin' north on Wentworth Avenue now. Quiz the garage man and come right in? Yis sor. Good-bye."

He turned to the office man, a pale, slightly built fellow with furtive, shifty eyes.

"Who owns that car that just backed out av here?" he asked.

"I don't know. Wait here and I'll find out for you. The foreman hasn't turned in the ticket yet."

He went out into the garage and they saw him question a workman in greasy brown overalls.

"I don't like the look av that bird," said Rafferty. "He's got a bad eye."

"I've been thinking the same thing," replied Buell. "He was all ears when you were talking to the chief."

The office man came back presently, and they saw the workman walk toward the back of the garage.

"Foreman's down in the machine shop," he explained. "Sent a man after him. I can't leave the office, you know."

They sat down to wait. Presently the workman reappeared.

"The boss's busy grindin ' some valves on a rush job," he said. "Says for you two guys to come on down if you want to talk to him."

They followed the man to the back of the garage. He opened a rickety wooden door and held it for them to pass. A dark stairway yawned before them.

"Go ahead and I'll hold my flash for you," he said. "The stair light's burnt out and we're short of globes. You'll find the boss in the front end of the machine shop."

Rafferty hesitated. Then, apparently reassured, he shrugged his shoulders and started down the stairway. Buell followed, and the workman came behind him with the light.

Suddenly, just as Rafferty reached the foot of the stairs, Buell saw a cylindrical object flash out from the darkness at the right and crash on the Irishman's skull. An instant later something struck him a terrific blow on the back of the head, strong arms seized him from behind, and he was forced to the floor, half dazed, yet struggling to shake off his assailants.

The unequal contest was soon terminated. With hands and feet securely bound, a coarse gag in his mouth and a blindfold over his eyes he was half dragged, half carried for some distance, then lifted and thrown into what appeared to be a motor truck, for he heard the roar of the engine and felt the jolting of the vehicle as it whirled away.

CHAPTER 4
THE MUFFLED FIGURE

WHEN she was dragged into the car by her two abductors, Doris Lee fought gamely, but to no purpose. Buell's leap to the running board and his subsequent battle with the pock-marked man, in which he appeared to be gaining the upper hand, brought hope of a speedy rescue. Then the man who held her swung his blackjack into play. Horrified at sight of Buell's fall from the swiftly moving car, she attempted to scream, but a heavy hand was clapped over her mouth. She bit the hand, and her captor shook her roughly.

"Easy, Spud," cautioned the man with the pock-marked face. "Remember the boss said to treat her gentle."

"You can't hold a wildcat and treat it gentle," replied the man called Spud. "She bit clean through my hand. Pull down them side curtains and let's get busy. We ain't got much time."

They were out of the loop, now, and whirling along at breakneck speed, but Doris, crowded down on the cushions between the two men, could not tell in what direction. The pock-marked ruffian pulled down the shades, then took a light, tough cord from his pocket and bound her wrists.

"Hold still, lady, and you won't get hurt," he said. "Pull at them cords and they'll cut the skin from your wrists."

"Get busy with that gag and blindfold, Pock," grunted Spud.. "I ain't getting' enough jack out of this to pay me for losin' a hand."

"A bite from that little mouth ain't goin' to hurt you none. Hold her head up a little higher."

They forced a gag into her mouth, tied a white silk muffler over her eyes, and lifted her to a more comfortable position in the rocking tonneau. She pulled at the cords that held her wrists, and they cut her cruelly. The gag half choked her and the blindfold was so tight her eyes ached, but she had no way of protesting and realized that it was useless to struggle further.

After what seemed at least an hour of fast driving, every minute of which held both mental and physical torture for the girl, the car came to a sudden, shrieking stop.

The two men helped her out and she heard it speed away. Then they piloted her down a short flight of steps and paused before a door at which one of them knocked—a series of timed taps that revealed the use of a code of some sort. She heard the door open, was led forward through several more doors, and came to a stop at sound of a voice in front of her.

"Stop. You two can go no farther. Give the girl to me. It is the command of the High One."

"Where d'ya get that boloney, black boy?" It was the voice of Spud. "We ain't givin' this girl to no nigger."

She heard the voice of Pock.. "It's all right, Spud. You're new at this game. The man's a eunuch and what he says is true. We can't go no farther. Ain't allowed."

"All right, you win. You been here a long time so you ought to know your onions."

Doris felt a large hand on her arm, and drew back with a shudder. The sound of retreating footsteps gradually dying in the distance told her the two men had left.

"Fear not, glorious one," said the voice beside her. "The skin of Barsar is black, but the heart is loyal and his arm is strong. He will guide and guard you safely to the blessed portals of Karneter."

He removed the gag from her mouth, which was a great relief, and she requested that her bandage be loosened. This also was done. Then she heard a humming sound like that of hidden motors and her guide led her forward a few paces. Again the motors hummed and there was a sound behind her as if a heavy door or gate had slid into place..

Once more her guide led her forward. Presently

she found herself descending a stairway. And such a stairway! She thought they had traveled at least a mile down those steps when they reached a level floor once more.

Again she heard the droning hum of motors. As they progressed this humming sound recurred at regular intervals for a considerable distance. Then her guide stopped.

"Barsar can go no farther," he said. "From this point others will guide you."

Another came, a woman this time, to judge from the sound of her voice.

"Come, glorious one," she said, placing her hand on Doris' arm. "Let Thansor guide you through the portals of Karneter, the blessed."

The motors hummed once more. Then they walked forward and descended a flight of steps. At the bottom the guide helped Doris into what was evidently a vehicle of some sort, for it contained a cushioned seat and moved away noiselessly, swaying slightly from side to side.

For twenty minutes she rode in the soundless, swinging vehicle. When at length her guide helped her out, they climbed a flight of broad, stone steps, and entered a room which, judging from the echoes of their footsteps on the hard floor and the time it took to cross it, was quite large. There was a pungent fragrance in the air that reminded her of incense.

Passing into what was evidently a carpeted hallway, she was led for some distance farther, then a door was thrown open and she was piloted through it. It closed with a metallic clang.

"Sisa! Tirabel!" her guide called. "The glorious one has come. Attend her promptly, for the Lord of Karneter will soon be here."

The door opened and Doris heard the departing footsteps of her guide. Gentle hands on each side of her led her to a cushioned seat. Deftly, swiftly, the hands removed her bonds and blindfold. When she opened her eyes she saw that she was attended by two girls attired in garments of strange design—clinging, translucent fabric of light blue trimmed with gold. Their bare feet were shod with sandals of light blue leather. Both girls were quite pretty, each in her own way. The girl who had just removed her blindfold stood beside her. She was tall and willowy, with an olive complexion and glossy, jet-black hair. The other, the one who had removed her bonds, knelt before her, gently rubbing her wrists. She was smaller, more inclined to plumpness, and had a pink and white complexion and fluffy auburn hair. She was the first to speak.

"I am Tirabel, glorious one," she said. "Sisa and I have been sent here to minister to your wants. You must be tired after your journey to Karneter. Sisa will prepare a refreshing bath while I help you with your clothing."

WHILE she was being made ready for the bath, Doris had time for a detailed observation of her surroundings. She occupied a suite consisting of three rooms and bath. It was furnished lavishly, gorgeously, the predominating colors being blue and gold. Hangings were of blue velvet fringed with gold and decorated near the top with an irregular sprinkling of silver stars worked into the fabric. The lacquered furniture was grotesquely carved, representing lions, leopards, human-headed animals, and queer monstrosities that could scarcely be said to resemble either humans or animals.

After a luxurious scented bath in a sunken marble tub, and a brisk rubdown at the hands of Sisa, Doris was arrayed in light blue clothing and sandals similar to the costumes of the two girls but more richly ornamented. Then Tirabel bound her fluffy golden hair with a band of blue velvet which supported a glittering silver star above her forehead.

The two girls surveyed their handiwork with open admiration.

"Is she not lovely, Sisa?" murmured Tirabel.

"Almost too lovely to be real," replied Sisa. "Our mighty lord would not have chosen her, otherwise. It must be that she is the most beautiful woman in the upper and lower worlds."

Suddenly a loud knocking sounded at the door. Sisa opened it, and was confronted by a gigantic woman who wore metal breastplates and wristlets and a cuirass of chain mail. A huge simitar was belted to her waist and she carried a long spear. The light glinted from her burnished helmet as she stooped to pass through the doorway. She was as generously proportioned in width as in stature and the muscles of her bare arms stood out like those of a trained athlete. Grounding her spear, she looked down at Sisa and said in a deep, almost masculine voice:

"News comes that the High One has arrived. Is all in readiness?"

"All is ready," replied Sisa.

"Then depart, that the glorious one may receive her lord alone."

Bowing low before Doris, Sisa and Tirabel took their departure. The giantess backed out after them and Doris noticed an iron-barred gate standing ajar just beyond it. When the door was closed once more she heard the clang of the gate as it swung into place.

She pondered the words of the giantess: "That she may receive her lord alone." Someone, a man, a ruler of some sort, was coming to her rooms. Evidently she had been abducted by his order. Why? For what purpose? She shuddered as she thought of the possibilities.

Rushing to the nearest window, she drew back the blue silk curtains and looked out. It was barred with heavy rods of steel. Beyond, she saw what looked like a tropical garden, bathed in moonlight. She ran to the next window, then the two remaining ones. All were similarly barred. There remained only the door. Hurrying across the room, she opened it softly. The gate was in place, fastened with a huge padlock. Just in front of the gate stood the armed giantess. She shut the door without heed to the noise it might make, made a last, hopeless circuit of the rooms, and returning, sank down on a blue and gold couch in utter despair.

Tears came presently, and she buried her wet face among the soft cushions, weeping helplessly — hopelessly. Minutes passed — more than thirty of them — and with them the flood of her tears. Complete exhaustion claimed her and she lay back languidly, only keeping her eyes open and her faculties alert by a supreme effort of will.

The minutes dragged on in dreary procession. She was nearly asleep when suddenly she heard the grating of a key and the creak of the metal gate. Then the door opened softly and a tall figure, muffled from head to foot in a dark blue cloak, stepped into the room.

Too paralyzed with fear to so much as lift a hand, Doris gazed at the cloaked figure in wide-eyed horror. Above the folds of the cloak which concealed the lower part of the face, she saw a pair of eyes — glittering, cruel, hawklike — regarding her steadily. Heavy black eyebrows that met in a

Otis Adelbert Kline

straight line above the nose added to the fierceness of their expression.

She caught her breath sharply, then screamed in mortal terror, as the figure came swiftly toward her!

CHAPTER 5
A STRANGE ROOMING HOUSE

BUMPING about in the rattling, roaring motor truck, Buell's body soon became a mass of aches and bruises. His head throbbed terrifically from the blow he had received in the garage and the gag all but strangled him.

After what seemed an age of relentless jolting, the vehicle came to a stop. He was dragged out, swung to the shoulders of three men and carried up a short flight of steps. A door opened, and then several more as they progressed, and he was taken up what was evidently a winding stairway, the steps of which creaked when trod upon. Two more stairways were mounted, then he was carried a few steps farther and a door opened. His captors lowered him to the floor. Then they left him without a word. He heard them close and lock the door and walk away, their footsteps dying in the distance.

Buell's hands were bound in front of him, and he was testing the strength of his bonds when a loud, blood-curdling groan suddenly shattered the comparative stillness. He lifted his hands and dragged the gag from his mouth. Then he pushed back the blindfold, yet all was black around him.

A series of grunts in the direction from which the groan had come was followed by a string of forceful and picturesque Celtic invective.

"Rafferty," he called, "is that you?"

"Heaven be praised, yer alive then, Buell," came the response. "I thought maybe the dirty divvils had kilt you."

"Not yet. They put a goose egg on my head and trussed me up like a fowl on a spit."

"Goose egg, is it? The bump on me head feels as big as wan av thim dinnysaur eggs. Sure, I'd give me month's pay for wan good poke at the lubber that hit me."

"That makes it unanimous," agreed Buell, raising his bound hands to his throbbing head.

"Wonder what they're—hullo!" Rafferty paused to listen. "It's company we seem to be gettin'."

The sound of approaching footsteps grew momentarily louder. They paused near at hand. Then came the murmur of gruff voices, the jingle of keys, and the grating click of a lock. Buell was momentarily blinded by a flood of yellow light as someone pressed a switch.

A man grasped him roughly by the arm and jerked him to a sitting posture. He blinked and looked into the leering eyes of the man with the pock-marked face. Standing near by was a second ruffian, holding a tray of food and steaming black coffee.

"Set the chow down beside 'em, Bill," said the pock-marked one. "They slipped their gags and blindfolds so I guess they kin eat all right with their mitts tied."

"I'll dare yez to untie mine, the both of yez," growled Dan Rafferty.

"Shut yer face before I kick it in fer you," politely responded the one called Bill.

"It's a couple av cowardly gutter-rats yez are," replied Rafferty, undaunted.

Buell saw the fellow's face redden with anger. He put the tray on the floor and advanced threateningly, then drew back a heavy shod foot for a kick. Buell swung his bound legs just in time to trip the ruffian, who fell, sprawling and cursing, into the tray of food. Then the pock-marked man struck him a heavy blow in the face that sent him back to the floor. A free-for-all scrimmage followed. Rafferty had rolled to the assistance of Buell, only to be set upon by the cursing, food-smeared bruiser. The pock-marked man rained furious blows on Buell's unprotected face and body. He managed to roll out of reach for a moment, but the fellow plunged after him with an angry roar. The moment's respite had given Buell an opportunity to draw back his bound feet, and he now planted them in the pit of the man's stomach as he bent over. The force of that

Otis Adelbert Kline

kick sent him clear to the opposite wall, where he fell, doubled up like a jackknife, the wind completely knocked from his body.

Turning, Buell saw Rafferty suddenly slide his bound wrists over the head and shoulders of his assailant, pinning his arms to his sides in such a manner as to make it impossible for him to strike an effective blow.

"Atta boy, Dan!" he cried. "Hold him." Then he rose and hopped to the assistance of his companion.

"Hold him, is it?" replied Rafferty, tightening his gorillalike arms until his captive groaned with pain. "Sure I'll crack ivvery bone in his body if he makes wan move or lets out a peep. See if the cowardly spalpeen has a knife."

Buell searched rapidly with his bound hands. From one hip-pocket he extracted a blackjack—from the other, a wicked-looking case-knife. Then he promptly used the former on the ruffian, the latter on his comrade's bonds.

"I'll just cut the knots," he said, "and unwind the rest. We'll need these ropes.."

They worked so swiftly that in five minutes they had both men bound and gagged. The pockets of the one with the pock-marked face had yielded weapons similar to those of his companion, so both detectives were now armed.

"A foine-lookin' pair of cutthroats," said Rafferty. "I'd like to see thim whin they come to, but I guess we'd best be lavin'."

Buell opened the door stealthily and looked out. He saw a long, dimly lighted hallway.

"Come on," he said. "Now's our chance."

They switched off the room light and locked the door.

"We'll search the house," he continued. "Doris may be a prisoner here."

"Lead on, me bye," replied Rafferty with enthusiasm. "Another iligant little scrap like that will take the rust out av me joints."

A SEARCH of the entire floor they were on proved fruitless. Every room was not only deserted, but bare of furniture as well. All windows were boarded up with heavy planking, spiked to the frames. They found a broad, banistered stairway at one end of the hall and a small, spiral stairway at the other.

"Must have been a rooming house at one time," said Buell. "This is evidently the top floor, as the stairways end here. Let's try the next one."

They noiselessly descended the smaller stairway, stopped at the next landing and opened the door that led to the hallway. The odor of tobacco smoke and the sound of voices greeted them. These apparently issued from an open transom at their left.

"Wait here," whispered Buell, "and I'll take a peek through the keyhole."

He tiptoed softly to the door and looked through the narrow opening. Four men, a hard-looking lot, were seated at a table playing poker. There were glasses all around, and two half-emptied whisky bottles. The man opposite the door, a burly, bottle-nosed ruffian with a tattered cigar gripped between his teeth, tossed a chip to the center of the table.

"Open for a dollar," he said.

"Stay," said the next man.

The others threw in their hands.

"Only one customer?" The burly one looked disgusted. "This game is goin' flat. Wonder what's keepin' Pock and Bill."

"Dey went up to feed dem two amachoor dicks," replied the man across from him.

"Seems like they're takin' a hell of a long time to it. By the way, what's the boss gonna do with them two?"

"Croak 'em, I guess, if de chief dick don't come across. Dey framed Verkler dis afternoon. 'Phoned in de number of his bus and he got pinched. Sproul wrote McGraw a note and offered to trade him, two men for one."

"Ain't Sproul gettin' awful generous?"

"Not him. He got his orders from de big boss."

Buell rose and beckoned to Rafferty. The Irishman, bursting with curiosity, joined him.

"What the divvil's goin' on in there?" he whispered.

"Poker game. Now is a good time to search this floor."

Lights shone through the transoms above three other doors. All the rest were dark. They investigated the lighted rooms first. Two proved to be bathrooms. In the third, they saw a man seated on the edge of a bed taking off his shoes. Four of the dark rooms proved to be unoccupied bedrooms. A fifth was bolted on the inside. A sleepy growl came from within as Buell turned the knob.

"Whadda ya want?"

"Pardon me. Got the wrong door," replied Buell.

"Why doncha look where you're goin'?" was the polite rejoinder. "Wakin' a guy up at this hour of the night."

Rafferty grinned.

"Sure and that was a close call," he said. "Yez got away wid it good, though."

Buell tried the last door in a more gingerly manner. He found an empty bedroom.

Again they descended the spiral stairway. This time they found three doors at the bottom. One was outlined with yellow light. From beyond it came a metallic clatter and an odor suggestive of cookery.

"The galley — I mane the kitchen," said Rafferty.

He bent to look through the keyhole, but there was none. Then he found it was a swinging door. By pushing it open a little way he gained a view within. He let it carefully back into place, then rose.

"Couple av slant-eyed Chinks polishin' pots and pans," he whispered.

In the meantime Buell had tried the two other doors. One opened to a basement stairway — the other to a butler's pantry.

"Might as well explore this floor while we're here," he said. "Come on."

Beyond the pantry was a spacious dining room, elegantly furnished. From another room still farther on, light filtered through the portieres that spanned the double opening.

As they neared the portieres a bell tinkled in the room beyond. It rang again, long and insistently. Looking between the portieres, Buell saw a large living room, comfortably and tastily furnished. It was lighted by a single, shaded floor lamp. At the far end a servant in livery was opening the door. He admitted a man whose beaver hat and fur-collared topcoat were powdered with snow.

"Is Sproul in?" he asked, as the man relieved him of topcoat and hat.

"Yes, sir. Mr. Sproul is expecting you, I believe, sir."

The servant strode pompously to a curtained doorway at the right. As he drew back the hangings a shaft of light flashed into the living room.

"Mr. Melvin to see you, sir," he announced.

"Veil, show him in," came a querulous, high-pitched voice from the other side.

The visitor entered.. As the light struck full on his face, Buell recognized the man who had black-jacked him in the limousine on the night of Doris' abduction.

"Runnels." It was the querulous voice again.

"Yes, sir."

"Go into the entryway and close the inner door. I vant to speak privately mit dis gentleman."

"Yes, sir. Very good, sir."

Buell waited until the servant had shut himself in the vestibule.

"Let's go," he whispered.

They tiptoed stealthily to the curtained doorway and peered within. Two men sat facing each other across a massive walnut table. One was the visitor. Buell gave a start of surprize as he saw the half-turned profile of the other. It called up a vision of a café—two men seated at a table edging the dance floor. One wore a square-cut beard and smoked long, Oriental cigarettes. The other, middle-aged and portly, toyed with a highball glass, even as he now toyed with a small golden inkwell.. Buell saw the connection now. Sproul was the agent of the black-bearded man and this other, the man called Melvin, was a minion of Sproul.

CHAPTER 6
THE FATE OF A RENEGADE

"VELL, Melvin, haff you decided to stick mit us?" Sproul pushed the inkwell from him and folded his pudgy fingers.

"Stick, hell! I told you what I'd do last night. I'm through. I agreed to help you pull this job—you and Pock. Pulled it slick, didn't we? Gimme my jack and we'll part friends. You don't need to come this 'Stick with the gang' stuff on me. I'm no squealer. You know that."

"It ain't that you're a squealer." Sproul plucked at his watch-chain and drew a small emblem from his vest pocket—an emblem similar to that which Buell had torn from the man with the pock-marked face. The burnished disk glittered in the light as he held it aloft. "Ven you got vun of dese you swore a certain oath. Are you going to keep it?"

"Certainly I'm going to keep it. I've done my part. All I want is a square deal. You know the penalty for kidnaping. Even if I wanted to squawk do you think I'd be damned fool enough to put my own head in the noose?"

Sproul leaned back heavily, replacing the charm in his pocket.

"That ain't the point, Melvin. Mit us the law of nature holds. All life is progress. You can't stand still — you can't go back. To do so is death."

Melvin half rose in his chair, his lips drawn back from flashing teeth.

"You dare to threaten me?" he snarled. He did not see what Buell and Rafferty saw — a pudgy thumb pushing a button on the table leg. "Do you mean to say you've got the brass to sit there and threaten Spud Melvin, champion gunman of the toughest ward in Chicago?"

Sproul raised a deprecatory hand.

"Now, now! Vait a minute. Sit down. Did I say I vos threatening you?"

Melvin sat down. As he did so, Buell noticed two sections of a built-in bookcase at his back, opening up like doors — slowly, soundlessly. Within the dark opening a grinning, ebony face appeared. Then a giant negro, naked save for turban and loincloth, stepped silently out. In his hand was a huge simitar. Like a great black leopard stalking its prey, he crept up behind the unsuspecting man and stood with weapon upraised.

Sproul, cool as a cucumber, picked up a pen from the table and balanced it on his middle finger. Not by the slightest flicker of an eyelash did he betray his knowledge of the negro's presence.

　　　　　　　　　　　　　　Otis Adelbert Kline

"Melvin," he said. "I don't threaten you. A power greater than either of us—greater than I can tell you, threatens. As the humble mouthpiece of that power I giff you this last chance. Are you mit us?"

Melvin leaned forward, tensely, alert.

"Sproul," he replied, "I recognize no power on earth except the power of Spud Melvin to fight his way through. I'm giving you this last chance to play square with me. Either come through with my dough or beat me to the draw. You always carry a gun and you know my speed. What'll you have?"

Sproul twirled the pen between thumb and forefinger with an air of unconcern.

"I haft said my say. I'm through."

"Then so am I, " rasped Melvin. "See, here's my hand above the table. I'm giving you a chance."

Sproul dropped the pen. The heavy simitar flashed downward, shearing Melvin's skull to the bridge of the nose. He slumped forward without a sound.

"Take him out, Barsar," cried Sproul. His voice was again high-pitched and querulous. "Don't pull the blade out until you get him off the rug. I don't vant blood all over it."

In a moment the negro had disappeared in the opening with the body of Melvin. The bookcases slid back in place as slowly and noiselessly as before.

Sproul coolly selected a cigar from a lacquered humidor on the table, lighted it, and puffed reflectively. Suddenly he cocked his head to one side in a listening attitude. At the same moment Buell and Rafferty heard the clatter of heavy shoes. Someone was running toward them from the back of the house.

"Quick," said Rafferty. "Duck behind this sofy."

A large, overstuffed davenport slanted across the corner of the room nearest them. They barely had time to leap behind its broad back when a man dashed past and entered the library.

"The dicks is gone!" he gasped. "Tied up Pock and Bill and locked 'em in the room."

Buell recognized the voice of the bottle-nosed man.

"*Himmel!* They must be in the house yet. Haff you searched?"

" The boys are lookin' around now."

"Look eferywhere. Look in the basement—on the roof. They couldn't pass the guards. *Mein Gott!* It will mean our heads if they are gone! Go! Hurry! Don't stand there like a *verdammte esel! Ach!* I must tell the High One."

Again the fellow hurried past the davenport. They heard a door slam in the rear, and the muffled clatter of shoes on the stairs.

Buell poked his head above the davenport, then lowered it hurriedly. The butler was coming toward the library..

"Did you call me, sir?" he asked.

"Call you? No. Go back to the vestibule, lock the doors on both sides of you and have your veapons ready. The detectifs are loose."

"Yes, sir. Right away, sir."

As soon as the butler closed the door, Buell and Rafferty emerged from hiding and approached the library. Looking between the curtains, Buell saw the two bookcase sections slowly swinging into place. Sproul was not in sight.

"He's gone," cried Buell, "through that hole in the wall. Come on."

They dashed into the library just as the sections settled into position. Buell pressed the button on the table leg and they swung slowly forward once more. An inspection of the dark opening revealed a small landing and a narrow stairway, descending steeply in front of them.

They stepped within. Voices came from the direction of the dining room.

"How're we gonna shut this thing?" inquired Rafferty. "Them roughnecks are comin' from upstairs."

Buell, looking around hastily, noted a small button on the ceiling, similar to that on the table leg. He pressed it, saw that the doors were closing, and led the way down the narrow stairs.

CHAPTER 7
WALLS WITH EARS—AND VOICES

THE two detectives, expecting to arrive in the basement with a comparatively few steps, were surprized to find that the stairway led on and on as if headed for the very center of the earth.

"Mebby this is the way them two Chink cooks came up," said Rafferty. "A couple av miles more and we'll be in their counthry."

"Can the comedy," advised Buell, who was a few steps in the lead. "I see a light ahead of us."

A hundred feet more and they were under the light, standing on a small, square landing. Facing them on three sides were stone walls. The floor and ceiling were of solid concrete. Their way was blocked in every direction except that from which they had come.

Rafferty, always inquisitive, tapped on the wall with his knuckles.

"Now what the—?"

He was interrupted by a voice, the deep, sepulchral tones of which sent cold chills racing up and down his spine and rendered him momentarily speechless. It echoed through the small enclosure without seeming to come from any particular part of it.

"What seek ye here?"

Buell was rendered as tongue-tied as his garrulous companion for a moment. Then a happy thought struck him.

"We have a message for the High One," he said.

There was a sound like the whir of a powerful motor, and the wall in front of them slid swiftly upward, revealing a dimly-lighted passageway beyond, but no sign of a human being.

"Proceed," said the mysterious voice.

Buell went ahead with inward misgivings but no outward sign of trepidation. Rafferty, close behind, seemed actually to be enjoying himself. He looked back as the wall dropped into place once more.

"Begorry, this is gettin' interestin'," he said. "Sure I've often heard that walls had ears, but I nivver even dreamt that they had voices."

Some distance farther on they reached another blank wall. They were interrogated in the same manner, gave the same answer, and were allowed to proceed as before.

They had passed a third, a fourth and finally a fifth wall when Rafferty began to show signs of misgiving.

"Mark me words there's somethin' spoiled in

Copenhagen," he said.

"It's beginning to look that way," replied Buell.

"Sure, it's all too aisy to be true. I'm beginning to think this place is a damned sight aisier to get into than out of."

They reached a sixth wall presently, and were interrogated as at the previous ones.

"What seek ye here?"

A peculiarity that Buell had noticed was that the voice at each wall not only repeated the same words as at the first one, but spoke in exactly the same tones, as if one man were conducting all the questioning.

"We bear a message to the High One," replied Buell, waiting for the wall to rise. He heard the whir of hidden motors, but the wall remained where it was. What could be happening? he wondered. He turned and saw that another wall had been lowered close behind them. They were hemmed in a narrow boxlike space.

Both men looked around apprehensively. There was no sign of a person or even an opening in any direction.

The stillness was suddenly shattered by a horrible shriek of demoniac laughter, which echoed and re-echoed from the walls of their prison.

"Laugh, you blisterin' hyena," shouted Rafferty. "Remimber he who laughs last gets the most fun out av it."

A horrid cackle answered him.

At the same moment Buell became conscious of a peculiar acrid odor permeating the enclosure and growing stronger every minute. With the coming of this odor it seemed that the room was beginning to rock gently to and fro as if it were swinging on the end of a long rope. Noting that the light was growing dim, he looked upward toward the small incandescent globe. A cloud of thick yellow vapor had partly obscured it.

"Fire!" he shouted. "The room is on fire!"

He could not hear the sound of his own voice. Instead he saw with horror that flaming letters were issuing from his mouth, spelling out the words and disappearing with puffs of yellow smoke.

The room was beginning to rock with more and more violence. In attempting to steady himself he collided with Dan Rafferty, who was similarly employed.

"Steady, me lad." The flaming words issued this time from the mouth of Dan Rafferty, visible but not audible.

With a supreme effort, Buell pulled himself erect. Suddenly he felt himself growing very rapidly. He was as tall as the Woolworth Building. Far below him Rafferty, looking no bigger than an ant, was holding out both hands and endeavoring to balance himself as if walking a tightrope. He felt himself growing smaller once more. Down, down he shot, with a swiftness that was appalling. The wind whistled past his ears and a sinking feeling similar to that experienced by some people in rapidly descending elevators attacked the pit of his stomach.

The next instant Dan Rafferty assumed gigantic proportions and Buell felt as small as an insect. The room began whirling, slowly at first, but gradually gaining momentum until an appalling speed had been attained. He kept to his feet with difficulty that increased as the whirling grew swifter. At length, reaching the limit of his endurance, he fell to the floor. A shower of multicolored sparks dropped around him. Then all went black. . . .

WHEN Doris Lee cried out in terror, the muffled figure approaching her couch stopped. Then a voice issued from the cloak.

"Come, Thansor, attend the girl. She seems hysterical."

A pudgy female, attired in a stiff blue robe trimmed with silver, came through the door. She threw back her cowl as she entered, revealing a shaven head and a round, moonlike face, the fat, puffy cheeks of which almost hid her tiny pig eyes.

She approached the couch and placed a moist, plump hand on Doris' brow.

"Be not afraid, glorious one," she said. "I am Thansor, who piloted you through the gates."

The muffled figure spoke once more.

"Give her the best of care, Thansor. I will go, now, and return when she is in a calmer mood."

Thansor made deep obeisance as the figure departed. When the door had closed and the gate clanged shut behind it, she turned once more to Doris.

"It was a mistake for you to receive our mighty lord in this fashion," she said. "You had naught to fear, for he merely wished to make sure you were the right girl."

Still trembling from the shock of her terrifying experience, Doris looked up into the little piglike eyes.

"The right girl for what?"

"There, there. We shall not talk of it tonight. You have been chosen, among all the beautiful women of the earth, for the greatest honor that can come to any woman. Tomorrow you shall know. Tomorrow, when you have rested and grown stronger, I shall instruct and prepare you. Let me help you to bed now."

The appearance of the bed to which the woman led her was not exactly conducive to peaceful slumber. It was supported by two lean, fierce-looking hunting leopards, carved from hard wood and lacquered orange and black.

When, however, she had donned her sleeping garment and crept beneath the covers, she found it more downy and comfortable than she ever imagined a bed could be.

For a long time—it seemed several hours—she lay there tossing restlessly, the pudgy, blue-robed figure at her bedside, but outraged nature finally asserted itself and sleep claimed her.

CHAPTER 8
THE HALL OF THE TWO TRUTHS

T HE first thing that smote Alan Buell's returning consciousness was a feeling of nausea
and an intense thirst. He craved cold, clear
water — buckets of it, barrels of it, whole rivers and
lakes of it. His tongue was swollen and furry, his
lips were parched and hot, and he discovered, as he
sat up to look about him, that every muscle in his
body was the seat of a separate, distinct, and intensely painful ache. Another discovery was even
more of a shock. On leaning forward to arise he was
brought up with a jerk by a stout chain attached to a
heavy metal collar that circled his neck. The other
end was fastened to a ring in the rough stone wall
behind him. Similarly fettered, Dan Rafferty was lying near by, snoring lustily.

The room was of stone — floor, walls and ceiling.
A grated steel door admitted light from what was
evidently a corridor without.

A heavy, measured tread sounded in the corridor. Presently a man passed the door. Buell gasped
in amazement when he saw that the man was not

only a giant, nearly seven feet in height, but that he wore the uniform of a soldier of ancient Egypt. In his right hand he carried a long, heavy spear. A sharply curved simitar dangled from the left side of his belt.

Dan Rafferty, awakened by the clatter, sat up and clasped his head in his hands.

"Oh, what a headache!" he groaned. "They've chained us up like a couple av dogs, too, the blitherin' swabs."

"What do you suppose they doped us with?" asked Buell. "It was like a mixture of white lightning, quinine and T. N. T."

"Acts like some dope I wance got in a joint in Port Said," replied Rafferty. "It was me buddy, Tim Rourke, got me to go into the place. The effect was the same, only we ate the stuff instid of inhalin' it. 'Hashish' is what them Naygurs called it."

"It gives you a queer bunch of hallucinations."

"An' a hell av a mornin' after. Sure, I feel as if a herd av wild elephants had been playin' follie-the-leader on me frame."

Fully an hour elapsed before anyone entered their cell.. Then a negro, clad in a turban, loin-cloth and sandals, brought them food on a tray. He was admitted by the giant guard, who stood with spear held in readiness for a thrust while the food was placed on the floor. It consisted of some round, hard biscuits, dried dates, and a cup of water apiece.

Buell's stomach rebelled at the sight of food, but he drank the water eagerly. Rafferty, whose gastronomic ability seemed unimpaired, munched his biscuits and dates and sipped his water sparingly.

"A foine layout of chow they hand you in this callyboose," he remarked. "It wouldn't kape a guinea-pig alive, much less a human."

"Take mine, too, if you want it," said Buell. "I can't even bear to look at it."

"It's lucky I am with a seaman's stomach," replied Rafferty, "that is, providin' I can manage to get it dacently filled now and then."

He consumed the second plate of food and, apparently much refreshed, amused himself by trying his strength on the staple to which his chain was fastened, at odd moments when the tall guard was out of hearing.

Buell, more sick than ever from having the water, tried to get some sleep. He was just falling into a doze when the lock clicked and the cell door was flung wide. Four men, each over seven feet tall, and dressed and armed like their guard, entered. They were followed by another, armed only with a simitar, who seemed to be in command. He ordered both detectives handcuffed — then took a bunch of keys from his girdle and unlocked the metal collars that held them. Each man was then led away between two guards.

THEY were hustled through a maze of arched, dimly lit corridors, and halted at length in what appeared to be a rather large anteroom. Three other prisoners, guarded and handcuffed like themselves, were lined up before a closed door. Two were dressed in ancient Egyptian costumes. The third wore the clothing of modern civilization.

After a wait of perhaps fifteen minutes two raps sounded at the door. A guard, opening it a little way, held whispered conversation with someone on the other side, then holding one hand aloft, he announced:

"It is the command of the mighty Osiris, Son of the Setting Sun and Lord of the Nether World, that these wandering souls be brought before him in the Hall of the Two Truths, where his righteous judgment will be passed on them."

He swung the door wide, all lights were extinguished, and the prisoners were led forward in utter darkness. Buell, the last in line, heard the door close after him. A moment later his guards brought him to a halt and he heard the butts of their spears as they grounded them on the stone floor.

Straining his eyes in the inky blackness, Buell at length beheld a tiny phosphorescent pinpoint of light a considerable distance ahead of him. It was round at first, but as it grew he noted that it spread more rapidly from side to side than from top to bottom, until it took on the shape and semblance of a flashing human eye a foot and a half in width. Beneath the eye another point of light glowed and grew momentarily larger. Gradually, eerily, a white-clad human form was revealed, seated on a massive, jewel-encrusted throne. On the head was a dazzling white crown adorned with plumes and horns and fronted with a burnished golden disk. In the hands, held crossed against the breast, were a shepherd's crook and a three-lashed whip. What attracted his attention the most, however, was the face—impassive, yet conveying the impression of concealed craft and cruelty. The eyebrows were heavy, overshadowing the glittering black eyes, and met in a straight line above the aquiline nose. Jaws and lips were clean-shaven except at the point of the chin, from which a long, narrow, tightly waxed beard curved downward and outward like the inverted blade of a sickle.

Something about the face—the expression—seemed strangely familiar. Buell racked his brain in an effort to recall where he had seen it before. Then his attention was attracted by a new demonstration. A beam of bright light shot suddenly from the pupil of the huge eye, making a brilliant white circle on the floor before the throne. Into the circle stepped a weird figure with a hideous jackal mask, and bowed low before the white-crowned ruler, who asked:

"What would you, Anubis?"

"The prisoners are ready to be judged, mighty Osiris."

"Then bring them forward, one at a time."

The jackal-masked Anubis advanced on the prisoners, followed by the circle of light. Roughly seizing the first man—the one who was dressed in the raiment of modern civilization—he dragged him before the throne and forced him to his knees.

The circle of light widened and two more masked figures stepped forward. The head of one was covered by a hood, fronted with the head and neck of an ibis. The other wore a hawk-mask before his face and a similar hood over head and neck. The man with the hawk-mask stepped up beside the prisoner.

"Mighty Osiris," he said, "I present Ammut, who was called Samuel Whitford the banker in the upper world. I charge him with having attacked his conductors with the intent to do them bodily injury while they were guiding him, at his own behest, into the blessed realm of Karneter."

The ibis-masked figure, holding a strip of papyrus before him, wrote rapidly thereon as if making a record of the name and charges.

"Have you aught to say for yourself, Ammut?" The man on the throne transfixed the cowering prisoner with a stern glance.

"They put a hood over my head and I objected," he replied. "Then they beat me and put manacles on my hands. Was it for treatment such as this that I paid you a hundred thousand dollars? Is this the fate of those who give up their all to follow the teachings of Mezzar Hashin?"

The figure on the throne scowled darkly down at him.

"For you, Mezzar Hashin has ceased to exist," he said. "His temple is in the upper world. You are now in the realm of Osiris, Lord of Karneter. Had you been tractable when conducted hither you would have been given the post of high authority promised you. As it is, you must be punished."

He turned to the ibis-masked figure.

"Thoth, you will record for Ammut a year at the hand-pumps. At the end of that period he will again be brought before us. We have spoken."

With the short crook in his right hand he struck a gong beside the throne. Then, from out the darkness at the right, came the sound of deep-throated roars, screeches and growls. Two crouching figures, hideously masked and costumed, bounded into the circle of light. Their heads were covered with grinning crocodile masks. Necks and shoulders were encased in shaggy lion's manes, and arms and body down to the waist in the skins of the same beast. Below the waist appeared the rounded rumps, stubby tails, and clubbed feet of hippopotami. Roaring lustily, they seized the hapless prisoner and hurried him away into the darkness at the left.

The next prisoner was brought before the throne in the same manner by Anubis.

"Whom have we here, Horus?"

The hawk-masked Horus replied:

"Punjad, whom I accuse of stealing a bottle of wine from the cellars of the temple."

"What have you to say for yourself, knave?" thundered the Lord of Karneter.

The miserable man prostrated himself before the throne, admitted his guilt, and begged for mercy.

"Give him forty lashes!"

This time three of the grotesque roaring figures bounded into the light. Two of them removed the prisoner's upper garment and hurled him to the floor. The third, who carried a heavy whip with three lashes, cut viciously into the bared back of the writhing, shrieking victim again and again, while Thoth counted and recorded the strokes. The shrieks died down to low moans before the thirtieth stroke, and ceased before the thirty-fifth as the man swooned, but the whip cut mercilessly on at the mangled, bleeding back until the sentence was completed. Then the limp body was dragged out into the darkness at the left.

Anubis conducted the third prisoner before the throne.

Again Horus stepped into the circle of light.

"Mighty Osiris," he said. "I present Jethlo, guard of the most holy Temple of Re. I charge him with profaning the sanctuary by improper advances to the vestal virgin, Delra."

The Lord of Karneter glared down at the prisoner.

"Do you deny this, wretch?" he roared.

The accused man did not grovel like the one who had gone before him.

"I did but present her with a bauble — a locket which she greatly admired," he replied.

"So! You have betrayed a trust and profaned the sanctuary of our Father by casting covetous eyes on a holy virgin."

He struck the gong and two of the hideously masked creatures again bounded into the circle of light.

"My faithful. Am-mits, you will take this vile wretch to Sebek, who will convey him to that inner Karneter whence no man returneth."

The circle of light moved backward from the throne, following the steps of the prisoner and his two weird conductors. Though he evidently knew what was coming, he did not flinch or falter, but walked forward with head erect and lips set grimly.

Presently the light flashed back from tall brass bars surrounding a circular pool of water about twentyfive feet in diameter. As the three men paused before a barred gate, Buell noticed the phosphorescent gleam of a pair of eyes and the glint of a wet snout in the water. One of the conductors opened the gate, the other pushed the prisoner within, and it was shut with a clang. There followed a sudden rush through the rippling water. Then the yawning, tooth-filled jaws of Sebek, the sacred crocodile, opened and snapped at their victim. He leaped back and ran around the edge of the pool, only to be felled by a blow from the powerful tail.

A moment later a few bloody bubbles marked the spot where he had been dragged beneath the water.

Again the circle of light swung back before the throne and rested on the solitary figure of the jackal-headed Anubis.

"How many prisoners remain?" asked the Lord of Karneter.

"There are but two, mighty Osiris. Those who were detectives in the upper world."

"They came together seeking admittance to Karneter. Bring both that we may judge them together."

Buell, manacled and helpless in the grip of his giant guards, had a feeling of impending doom as the repulsively masked Anubis advanced in the moving circle of light.

AS BUELL and Rafferty were led before the throne, the former again scanned the face of the man seated thereon. The closer view brought full recognition. He was the man of whom Doris Lee had been in mortal fear at the opera and later at the café, from in front of which she had been abducted. Evidently he had worn a heavy false beard and mustache both to serve as a disguise and to cover the odd, sickle-shaped beard which would have made him conspicuous anywhere in Chicago.

Horus of the hawk-mask stepped into the circle of light.

"Mighty Osiris," he proclaimed, "I present Dan Rafferty and Alan Buell of the upper world. They sought admittance at the gates of Karneter, saying that they bore a message to the High One."

The man on the throne looked down at them from beneath beetling brows.

"We await the message," he said.

The ibis-masked Thoth poised his pencil expectantly.

Rafferty looked at Buell and Buell looked back at Rafferty. There was a moment of ominous silence.

" Quick! The message!" snapped Horus.

Buell gazed defiantly throneward. "I demand the immediate release of my fiancee, Doris Lee," he said.

A sneering smile curled the lips of the potentate.

"A jackal may demand his mate from a lion," he replied, "and as readily gain the favor. Your insolence is in keeping with your rashness in entering Karneter. Know you, then, that she who was Doris Lee in the upper world exists no more as such. She is being prepared for the ceremony which will be the crowning event of the great Festival of Re four days hence, when she will become Isis, bride of Osiris, and co-ruler with him of the blessed realm of Karneter. But enough of this. We must to business. He who was Dan Rafferty will henceforth be called Baku. He has been an electrician, a policeman, a sailor and a detective. Put him to work at his first occupation."

"Now how the divvil did yez know I was a trouble-shooter fer the Western Electric?" he exclaimed.

"Silence!" commanded Horus. "The mighty Osiris sees all — knows all."

The potentate struck the gong and two roaring, hideously masked Ammits leaped into the circle of light. They seized Dan Rafferty and hurried him away, leaving Buell with Anubis, Horus and the scribbling Thoth.

"As for him who was Alan Buell, in the upper world," said the potentate when the roaring had subsided, "his name shall be 'N.' We have selected him for the high honor of impersonating the Osiris N at the Festival of Re."

"May I ask," queried Buell, "the reason for this unmerited kindness?"

" 'Tis but a trifling thing, and will soon be ended," was the reply. "Before the festival is over you will have entered that inner Karneter whence no man returneth."

"You mean I am to be killed?"

"Precisely, but there is nothing about that for you to be greatly concerned over. You will not know when the blow is struck, nor will you know aught afterward, so far as this physical world is concerned."

He smote the gong and the noisy Am-mits rushed Buell off into the darkness.

CHAPTER 9
DELRA, VESTAL VIRGIN

WHEN Dan Rafferty was dragged out of the Hall of the Two Truths he thought he emerged in bright sunlight. One of the Am-mits summoned a giant soldier who lolled at the entrance with a score of companions and handed him a strip of papyrus. After scanning the characters thereon, the fellow removed Rafferty's manacles and led him away. They were walking the streets of a city that reminded Dan of the Orient with its flat-roofed buildings and gaudily attired inhabitants; yet somehow it was different. It was almost as if he had been conveyed to another world. Even the blue vault of heaven above him seemed unnatural — almost unreal. The sun, too, had an artificial look. Mystified, he hurried on.

They passed through a noisy bazaar wherein was displayed a great variety of merchandise — shimmering silks and satins of a thousand brilliant hues, rare tapestries, rugs, bric-à-brac, jewelry, dried fruits, sweetmeats, perfumes, crockery, baskets — a hodgepodge of things Eastern over the prices of which busy merchants haggled spiritedly with thrifty purchasers.

Beyond this was a more quiet street in which half-naked children romped. Here and there Rafferty observed veiled women peering curiously down at him from latticed windows.

They came at length to a great rugged building from the interior of which issued sounds familiar to the ears of Dan Rafferty — the whirring roar of enormous electric generators. The soldier turned him over to a portly, red-faced individual who rolled up his sleeve and locked a steel armlet, on which a number was imprinted, just above his elbow. He was then guided by a second man, a guard with a spear and simitar, into what appeared to be a sort of dormitory. His guide showed him to a sleeping alcove, above the curtained entrance of which was a number corresponding to that on his armlet. An attendant brought a dull blue one-piece garment that left arms and shoulders bare and came down to the knees; also a pair of sandals. These he was commanded to don. His own wearing apparel was then taken away and he was conducted through a series of rooms and corridors to a quiet, soft-spoken individual who evidently had considerable authority. Here he was questioned about his previous experience as an electrician and, on divulging that he had been a troubleshooter, was given a set of tools and an assignment.

"They have been having trouble with some light switches in the Temple of Re," said the soft-spoken person. "Seboul, here, will conduct you thither and help you repair them."

He motioned to a beardless youth, dressed and outfitted like Rafferty.

"Seboul," he said, "this is Baku, a new slave in the Department of Electricity. You will go with him to the Temple of Re and assist him in repairing the switches."

Seboul bowed solemnly.

"We go at once, master," he replied. "Come, Baku."

"Baku!" muttered Rafferty as they passed out the door and down the street. "And they hand me that in place of an honest Irish name!"

"Pardon?" queried Seboul.

"I was just sayin'," replied Rafferty, "that it's an uncommon foine day."

"Not uncommon.. We always have good weather in Karneter."

"Do yez, now? I was noticin' somethin' peculiar about the sky, and the sun, too, for that matter."

"No doubt they could be improved," said Seboul. "In fact they only reached their present state of perfection a few years ago. When the great-grandfather of the present Lord of Karneter founded the city one could see the joints where the glass was fastened together. The sun, moon and

Otis Adelbert Kline

stars were then moved by man-power, too, but all this has been done away with. The second Lord of Karneter discovered a method of welding the sheets of glass together so they now appear as one piece, and the third inaugurated the system of moving all heavenly bodies with electric machinery. He also improved and perfected the rays of the sun to such a degree that flowers, plants and trees thrive as well as in the upper world."

"Yez don't tell me, now! The heavens sort of runs by clockwork, so to speak. Begorry, whoever doped that out had some head on him."

"Mezzar Hashin the First was a great prophet, teacher and scientist," replied the youth. "My grandfather, who knew him personally, has told me much about him."

"Yer grandfather? Yez don't mane to tell me you've lived all yer life underground!"

"Not only I, but my father and grandfather before me. My great-grandfather came here with Mezzar Hashin, first Osiris of Karneter, when he founded this city."

"That must've been before the Civil War. They didn't know much about electricity then."

"Not in the upper world. But it is said that the wisdom of Mezzar Hashin the First, in things material as well as spiritual, far transcended that of all others of his time."

"Sure and he must've been a smart bozo. Begorry, that's a swell-lookin' structure we're comin' to—the wan wid the gardens and wall around it. What do yez call it?"

"That," Seboul replied, "is the Temple of Re."

A moment later they came before a tall iron gate. A guard stopped them while he jotted down the numbers of their armlets on a sheet of papyrus. Then his companion swung the gate back, admitting them to a beautiful garden in which were long stretches of velvety grass, patches of flowers and shrubs that bloomed luxuriantly, numerous chimps of date palms and fig trees, and limpid pools where sparkling fountains played.

As they followed the winding, tree-bordered path which led to the great white building in the center, Rafferty noticed a number of white-clad girls gathering fruits and flowers while a small group of their companions fired slim, gold-feathered arrows at a target, displaying considerable skill. Seboul informed him that they were vestal virgins. He also saw a few men with shaven heads, wearing yellow robes—priests of Re—and many blue-clad garden slaves.

At the pillared portico of the temple a guard stopped them and asked their business.

"We were sent to repair some defective switches in the temple," Seboul told him.

The guard pressed a button which rang a bell inside, and presently a yellow-robed priest appeared.

"It's time the Department sent repair men," he grumbled, on being informed of their business. "Come with me."

They followed him through a vestibule, and thence into a room, the size and magnificence of which dazzled Rafferty. It was rectangular in shape, with an arched ceiling, the top of which was fully a hundred feet above their heads. Large statues of the lesser Egyptian deities were placed at intervals along the frescoed walls, on which were depicted in bright colors, scenes of battle, of hunting and of sacrifice. At the far end of the room was a huge disk of burnished gold from which the rays of hidden lights were reflected in all directions. A thin spiral of smoke curled upward from an altar in front of the disk, while on the right and left, respectively, there were colossal images of Osiris and Isis. It was to the base of the latter that he led them. A battery of multicolored footlights, he said, refused to respond properly to the various switches, and they were to be used at services that very evening.

After putting Seboul to work cleaning and testing the bulbs in front of the image, Rafferty went around behind it and removed the wall plate which concealed the switch mechanism. The priest, after watching him for a moment, departed, grumbling about the inefficiency of the Department of Electricity.

DELVING into the bewildering array of wires and contact plates, Rafferty soon found the cause of the trouble—a short, due to faulty insulation, had burned out several fuses. He had retaped the exposed wires and was about to replace the fuses, when the sound of a light footfall behind him caused him to turn. His look of surprise turned to one of frank admiration as he gazed into a pair of big brown eyes turned covertly in his direction. Their owner, a graceful girl in the clinging white garments of a vestal virgin, instantly averted them and passed on toward the altar. He stared after her, enraptured.

"A peach!" he murmured. "An angel from heaven in this haythen place!"

His eyes took in the details of her costume as she poured powdered incense on the altar from a narrow, jewel-encrusted vase. Her jet-black hair was circled by a square-linked chain of ivory. A similar chain gathered her white garment to her slender waist. On her feet were sandals of soft, white leather.

Her task completed, she started back toward him. Dan saw that she was headed for a door behind the image. She smiled slightly as she approached, and he gathered courage to speak to her.

"Hello," he said. "Me name's Dan Rafferty, at your service."

She paused, looked quickly around her as if in

fear of being seen, then smiled once more, displaying a perfect set of dazzling white teeth.

"How interesting," she replied.

"Sure, and you're the most interestin' sight I've seen in ages," said Dan. "Won't yez tell me your name?"

"It's Delra," she answered, and turned to go.

"Faith, Delra, yez needn't hurry away."

"I must go at once. We might be seen."

"And then they'd feed me to the crocodile, would they?"

"They would."

"Same as Jethlo?"

Her face blanched.

"I was so sorry," she said, "but it was all his fault. He insisted on coming. Sessed saw him and told the High One."

"Who is Sessed?"

"One of the temple guards. He is very jealous of me, although I have never encouraged him. He is quite annoying."

"Tell me where to find him," growled Rafferty, "and I'll punch him in the eye."

"No, no! You would be whipped, and perhaps executed."

"I'm comin' to see yez again, just the same, Delra. By the way, do yez know of a girl hereabout named Doris Lee?"

"Do I know of her? Assuredly. She who was

Doris Lee in the upper world is to become Isis, Bride of Osiris, at the Festival of Re."

"Where is she now?"

"In the Temple of Isis, of course. She is being schooled and prepared for her part in the coming ceremonies. I must go now. I see Sessed coming and I think he is watching me. Good-bye."

"Good-bye, Delra."

Rafferty watched her until the softly-closed door shut her from view. Then he turned to his task with a sigh.

"Sure, that's a wonderful girl," he murmured, fumbling with the fuses. "But here I'm thinkin' all about mesilf and lavin' Buell out in the cold. He's got to find his girl, and she's in the Temple of Isis, whatever and wherever that is, and what's more, it's up to Dan Rafferty to help him. But first av all I've got to find Buell. It's wan divvil av a mess!"

Otis Adelbert Kline

CHAPTER 10
THE DEATH WATCH BEGINS

BUELL was conducted by the Am-mits to an inner chamber of the Temple of Osiris. It was a small room with a low ceiling, lighted at one end by two red lamps of grotesque pattern, one on each side of a huge individual who sat behind a small table.

"We bring the Osiris N," said the Am-mits in unison. Then they withdrew, leaving Buell alone in the center of the floor.

The features of the man behind the table were hidden by a jet-black mask, but it was evident that his head, concealed by a scarlet hood on which a grinning skull was perched, was enormous. His shoulders, too, covered with a garment of bright scarlet, were as broad as those of two men. He rose suddenly, the skull on his headpiece almost touching the ceiling.

"Welcome, Osiris N, to the gateway which leads to the inner Karneter," he said in a deep, rumbling voice. "I am Odd."

"You are, sure enough," thought Buell, but he

said nothing.

The huge fellow pulled a cord and two attendants entered. They removed Buell's clothing, wrapped a black garment about him, put a black hood on his head and shod him with black sandals. Then they left quietly, taking his clothing with them.

"Now that you are suitably attired I will show you about Karneter," rumbled the giant. "Then we will proceed with your training."

He unwound a stout chain from about his waist. One end was attached to a ring in his huge leather belt. The other he wrapped around the waist of Buell, drew it tight, and secured it with a padlock.

"Come," he said.

They walked out side by side, the giant stooping as he passed through the door. Each man held up a portion of the six feet of chain between them.

"Why the chains?" asked Buell. "It seems to me that they are unnecessary."

"It is the law of Karneter," replied the giant. "The N must be bound to Odd until sunrise on the day of the Festival of Re.,"

"Sort of death watch, I suppose."

"You might call it that, though I have never heard the expression."

After traversing a maze of halls and passageways they came to a long, curved corridor much wider and taller than the others. At intervals of about a hundred feet along the wall at the right were circular openings some twenty feet in diameter. These were covered with heavy netting and in each of them a huge fan with eight-foot blades roared sonorously.

"These are the ventilators that bring air to Karneter from the upper world," explained Odd. "Far above us are others, revolving in an opposite direction, which draw out the foul air."

"Funny I've never seen or heard of any of the outlets," said Buell.

"You wouldn't. They are through buildings that have been built or purchased for the purpose. Some are houses with open inner courts. Others are factory buildings with tall chimneys that never smoke. All air is filtered, sterilized by heat, and then cooled and given the proper amount of moisture before it comes through those openings. The air in Karneter is, therefore, purer than that of the upper world—the large cities in particular."

Buell was impressed, but it was not until he had been taken out under the artificial sun and sky and had learned its history that he began to have some realization of the power and resources of the man against whom he had pitted his relatively puny strength.

"At night," said Odd, "the moon, stars and planets will come out and move across the sky, just as they do in the upper world. The only apparent difference to the naked eye will be that the skies are always cloudless. Tonight I will show you the ruddy Mars, due south, the full moon rising in the east, and blue-white Jupiter just ready to drop below the horizon in the west. We will watch the progress of the big dipper as it circles the North Star. Rising early in the morning we will see Saturn winking craftily down at us, followed by the silver-hued Venus, gliding along the plane of the ecliptic — the brilliant herald of the rising sun."

"Marvelous!" exclaimed Buell.

"Also," continued Odd, "with the aid of a telescope you can follow the movements of Mercury, Uranus and Neptune. You can see the moons that circle the planets, the beautiful, wraithlike nebulæ, and the double stars. When a comet comes to visit the solar system its appearance and movements are watched and duplicated here."

"But why this elaborate duplication of the terrestrial heavens?" inquired Buell.

"Our priests are both astronomers and astrologers. They could not properly conduct their holy offices without making their daily and nightly observations. It is a necessary part of the religion of Re. The appearance of the sky from the outer world is communicated to our master star-controller from our two secret observatories in the upper world, at stated intervals by telephotograph. On cloudy nights there are, of course, no telephotographs, but

the appearance of the sky as it should look is duplicated here just the same."

"I can not understand," said Buell, "why any individual or group of individuals should take the
trouble to build an artificial world when there are
vast uncolonized areas where this trouble would
not be necessary. A city such as this might be
founded in Africa or South America without a
fourth of the trouble, labor and expense involved
here."

"Mezzar Hashin the First planned a city that
would endure," replied Odd, "a city that would re-
tain its identity and traditions though kingdoms fall
to the swords of the conquerors, empires crash and
disintegrate, and even the mighty republics fade
away. Every nation of which we have historic re-
cords had a period of growth which, if not cut off
before its time, reached a climax of great splendor
and power, then crumbled with decay from within
or was crushed by stronger peoples from without.
On the ground above our heads people live in peace
and plenty in the second city of the greatest repub-
lic in the world. They may continue thus for a half-
century, a century even, but as a city, they are
doomed, even as their nation is doomed. Some day
they will reach their climax of splendor and
power—lean, jealous, hungry hordes will rush in
from Asia or Europe, perhaps both, and the proud
people of America will bow their necks to the yoke

of the conqueror."

"You are wrong, Odd," replied Buell, vehemently. "They would have to kill the last male able to bear arms before my people would surrender their liberty."

The giant smiled, the smile of one who is tolerant because of superior knowledge and power.

"History repeats itself," he said, "and every nation on the face of the earth is doomed. With us in Karneter it is different. No other nation knows of the existence of this city, which is growing rapidly — will soon be a nation, in fact, both in extent and in point of numbers. We are not troubled by wars, floods, drouths, storms, famine or pestilence. What we want, and can not obtain or manufacture here, we take from the upper world by means of our clever agents. They work with us for a price, yet even they do not know of our existence. Great quantities of gold, silver, jewels and other valuables disappear from the huge sleeping country above us, never to be recovered. Crime rings, gangsters, and others of their ilk are blamed, but our agents are seldom caught. When caught, they do not tell for whom they are working for the simple reason that they do not know. Beautiful girls and women vanish, hundreds of them a year, and are never heard from again. The white slave traffic is usually blamed and each incident soon forgotten by the public.

"Our trusted priests are establishing temples in all parts of the world like the one conducted by Mezzar Hashin in Chicago. Brains, beauty, wealth and power come to us through these sources. People adopt our religion and renounce the upper world without knowing where or what Karneter really is, for religion is an emotional, rather than a logical thing—a thing of faith rather than of knowledge. Some regret their decisions when first introduced here, but our mighty ruler has ways of making good subjects of most of them. Those who refuse to submit gracefully to our laws and customs are put at hard labor, which eventually cures or kills them."

WHILE they were conversing, Buell's guide was leading him through the most populous district of Karneter, and he marveled, as Rafferty had, at the size and metropolitan aspect of the place.

After they had visited the busy bazaar they circled through a beautiful portion of the residence district and came before the magnificent Temple of Re. While the giant Odd was conversing with one of the guards at the gate, who appeared to be an old friend, two men in blue costumes of slaves showed their numbers and passed through. Buell, who was standing several feet behind Odd, caught his breath sharply as he saw that one of the men was Dan Rafferty.

"Dan," he cried, "what are you doing here?"

"Hist!" Dan waited until his companion had gone on ahead. "I just learnt that yer girl is in the Temple of Isis. She's going to marry — "

Buell felt a tug at the chain that circled his waist. A deep voice boomed in his ear.

"Come, N. We will visit the Temple of Re. Do not debase yourself by talking to mere slaves. Remember that you are soon to be a god."

Buell scarcely noticed the marvelous gardens, the wandering vestal virgins, yellow-robed priests and blue-clad slaves. The richly and artistically designed temple which would ordinarily have aroused his interest and admiration elicited only absent-minded "yes's" and "oh's" as Odd enthusiastically pointed out this or that object of reverence and related the history of the building.

When they had passed out into the garden and were headed for the gate once more, Buell said, "There are other temples in Karneter, I presume."

"Only two. The Temples of Osiris and Isis."

"Are we to visit them?"

"You have already been in the Temple of Osiris. In fact that is where we are quartered. You did not see the grounds and gardens because we left through an underground passageway. The Hall of the Two Truths where judgment was passed on you is the main room in the Temple of Osiris. It is always kept in darkness, the only light coming from

Otis Adelbert Kline

the throne itself or the eye above it when the mighty Osiris is present to dispense justice."

"And the Temple of Isis?"

"It is some distance from here. Would you prefer to visit it today, or seek rest and refreshment now and leave it for another day?"

Buell did not want to appear overanxious. On the other hand, he certainly didn't want to pass up a chance to learn where Doris was quartered and catch sight of her if possible—perhaps converse with her.

"Let's clean up this round of the temples today," he said. "It will give us more time for rest and study tomorrow."

"Good. This way, then."

CHAPTER 11
THE MAN IN THE DUNGEON

BACK at their quarters in the power house, Rafferty and Seboul, in company with a number of other blue-clad slaves of the Department of Electricity, partook of a hearty meal consisting of stewed beef and mushrooms, date bread, and black Arabian coffee. The Irishman was surprized to learn that everything, even the beef, had been grown in Karneter.

"We have pastures and fattening pens in the south end of the city," explained Seboul. "As for mushrooms, there are none produced in the upper world that can compare with ours in size, excellence of flavor or vigor of growth."

After the meal the men rose and filed past a guard who noted their numbers and handed assignments to each. Rafferty read the neatly typed order on the strip of papyrus given him:

"Go to shaft seventy-four, guided by Seboul, and repair power circuit."

He turned to his comrade, who was engaged in deciphering his own order.

"Where is this shaft sivventy-four?" he asked.

Seboul shook his head.

"It's a bad place to work in," he replied. "The deepest of the new safety shafts in Karneter. If there is something wrong with the power circuit it means that it is rapidly filling with water, for they can't do much in that shaft with the hand-pumps. We must go quickly."

They picked up their tool kits and hurried out, following the same street they had taken that morning. To his surprize, Rafferty noticed that Seboul was again leading him to the Temple of Re.

"Haven't yez got yer wires crossed, lad?" he asked.

Seboul looked puzzled.

"I'm afraid I don't quite understand."

"Ain't yez headin' wrong? This is where we just came from."

"Shaft seventy-four is beneath the dungeons which are under the Temple of Re," explained Seboul.

They were stopped at the gate as before, and again at the pillared temple portico. Then the surly, yellow-robed priest who had been their guide that morning, conducted them to the rear of the temple, where Rafferty looked slyly about with the hope of seeing Delra, the vestal virgin. They descended a flight of winding stairs. Then the priest took them through an enormous basement in which were great quantities of canned and dried food and casks and bottles of wine. At the head of another stairway he halted.

"Follow these stairs to the third level below this," he said. "Then take the A passageway which leads to the main corridor of the top dungeon, follow it to the central stairway and descend thence to the seventh level, where you will find workmen who will direct you to the proper shaft."

"Mebby we better make a note av it," suggested Dan.

"That isn't necessary," replied Seboul. "Come. I will guide you."

They descended to the third level as directed, and Dan saw that the thing was not quite so complicated as it sounded. Three narrow passageways marked "A," "B," and "C," branched out from the foot of the stairs.

"Faith, it's simple as A, B, C," said Rafferty as they entered the A passageway.

"It isn't so simple farther down," replied Seboul, "but we'll find the way."

As they passed along the dimly lighted main corridor of the upper dungeon, Dan noticed the inmates of the cells. All were chained to rings in the walls with metal collars about their necks, just as he and Buell had been chained when they awoke in Karneter.

At the second level the rays of light grew feebler,

Otis Adelbert Kline

and ere they had passed the third they were compelled to use their pocket flashlights. On reaching the fourth level they were confronted by a confusing maze of corridors, cells and passageways. This was the deepest, darkest, and most feared dungeon in Karneter, according to Seboul. Prisoners sentenced to life imprisonment here usually begged for death sentences instead. There was no attempt at sanitation as in the upper dungeons, and vermin were allowed free range. The air was heavy with moisture and reeked with the stench of offal and the decaying bodies of those victims whom death had mercifully removed from this realm of frightfulness. The cells were irregular in form, more like crude caves, and there were no bars across them, though the chains and rings were much heavier and stronger than those which held the prisoners in the upper dungeons. As Rafferty and his companion hurried off down one of the passageways, their flashlights held before them and their handkerchiefs tied over their noses to filter the air they breathed, a dozen huge gray rats, disturbed at their business of devouring an emaciated corpse, showed their teeth and squealed menacingly. Dan caught a glimpse of the face. The lips, cheeks and end of the nose had already been eaten away. A rat was tugging at the blue-white tongue which protruded from the sagging, grinning jaws, while another nibbled hungrily at a glassy, lidless eye. The Irishman shuddered and passed on.

Suddenly, to his intense surprize, he became aware that Seboul was not with him. His pause, brief though it was, had separated them. Before him lay a half-dozen winding passageways, any one of which his fellow slave might have taken. He waited for a moment, then shrugged his broad shoulders and took the central one. Although it occurred to him to call, he hated to do this, as he did not want his companion to think him afraid, and felt confident that he could make his way alone.

He had gone but a short distance when he was startled by a sudden tug at his garment and a low voice at his side.

"Where to, slave? Only empty cells and gnawed bones lie beyond here. Are you lost?"

He turned and beheld a face that was wrinkled, ugly and emaciated. The prisoner, for such he was, as evidenced by the collar and chain, had been horribly mutilated—his right ear cut off and his right eye gouged out. His bony frame protruded here and there through rents in the filthy rags that had evidently once been yellow, and his clawlike hands trembled as he clung to Dan's garment.

"Sure and yez guessed it right," replied Dan, "but don't claw at me clothes like that. I won't run away."

The man released his hold on Dan's clothing.

"Your pardon, friend," he said. "It's so long since

Otis Adelbert Kline

I've seen a human being, other than the masked, voiceless guard who brings my food, that I could not bear to see you leave without a moment's conversation. Where did you say you were bound for?"

"Shaft sivventy-four, whatever that may be."

"I can direct you, but stay and talk yet a while. The work can wait and you have a good excuse."

"They say the damned thing's wid water," replied Dan. "Tip me off now, and I'll see yez whin I come back."

"You promise?"

"What're yez tryin' to do? Make a liar out av me?"

"Not at all. You appear honest. Go back to the first group of cross-passageways you find. Follow the second one to your right as you leave this one, and you will reach shaft seventy-four."

"Thanks. I'll be back as soon as I get the pumps to workin'."

DAN followed the directions of the mutilated prisoner, and was soon traversing the new passageway. He wondered what the fellow wanted of him. Was it merely companionship, or something else? Judging from the color of the rags that hung on his bony frame, the man had once been a priest. He was puzzling over the enigma when a light flashed some distance ahead of him and he heard someone shout, "Baku. Where are you, Baku?"

A moment passed before he remembered this was the name by which he was to be known in Karneter.

"Coming, Seboul," he replied. "Kape yer shirt an."

His fellow slave dashed breathlessly up.

"I have no cause for removing my shirt," he replied solemnly, "but we must hurry. The shaft is filling rapidly in spite of all the pumps that can be inserted. A score of workmen were drowned just before I arrived."

The two men ran down the passageway. Presently Dan saw lights ahead and heard the murmur of voices. A hundred feet farther on they came to a group of men working excitedly around a concrete-edged hole about fifteen feet in diameter.

"Here is the master electrician," shouted Seboul to a tall, beetle-browed man who was evidently an overseer.

The man looked Dan over.

"See what's wrong with that power circuit, and be quick about it," he ordered.

A half-dozen groups of slaves were working wildly at as many hand-pumps. The water they pumped out was apparently being forced to a higher level, as the pumps were connected with pipes which pierced the floor above. Disregarding these, Dan hurried to the power pump. He disconnected the two wires which led to the powerful motor and held the ends close together. A jagged spark sputtered across the intervening space.

"Nothing wrong with the circuit," he said. "Must be the motor." He examined the wiring underneath, found a loose connection, and had the motor humming in less than five minutes. The futile efforts of the hand-pumping crews were then discontinued and the overseer allowed the exhausted men a few minutes of rest before ordering them to disconnect their pumps.

Peering over the edge of the shaft, Rafferty saw the water, far below him, sinking steadily. Turning away, he noticed one of the slaves who seemed more exhausted than the others, lying flat on his back. He recognized Ammut, once Samuel Whitford the banker, who had donated a hundred thousand dollars to Mezzar Hashin when he joined his followers.

"What's the big hole in the ground for?" Rafferty asked Seboul as they stood beside the rapidly humming motor.

"It is one of the many safety shafts which the High One is sinking at various points in Karneter as a precaution against floods or leaks. At one point the waters of Lake Michigan are kept out only by walls of thick glass. In the event of a flood from that source or from any of the numerous springs which we are constantly damming with concrete, they will act as safety reservoirs for the water, and thus give us ample time to repair the leaks. This shaft is not completed and the workman at the bottom suddenly struck a huge spring. The motor on the power pump failed to work and many of the men were drowned. Their bodies are lying in the passageway across from us now, waiting to be conveyed to the crematory."

"Are all bodies burned in Karneter?" inquired Rafferty.

"No. Only those of slaves or others who can not afford caskets. The bodies of the wealthy are placed in leaden caskets and shot out into the lake with a special device we have for the purpose. The caskets are equipped with planes and propellers which carry them for a stated distance, when they sink to the bottom and are eventually covered by the drifting sand. But we waste time here, and the overseer is observing us. As the motor is now in working order we had best go back and report."

"Suits me," replied Dan. "I sure ain't crazy about this place."

They had traversed the long passageway and arrived at the six-point intersection, Seboul taking the lead as usual, when Rafferty was suddenly reminded of his promise to the imprisoned man. He hated to spend any more time in the stinking dungeon than was absolutely necessary, but being a man of his word, he halted, made sure that his companion had not observed him, and then

Otis Adelbert Kline

plunged silently down the passageway which he had previously taken by mistake.

CHAPTER 12
THE TEMPLE OF ISIS

BUELL and Odd, after leaving the Temple of Re, set out in what the former believed was a southerly direction. At least it was southerly by the bearings he took from the artificial sky, and he assumed that this corresponded to the directions in the upper world. If it didn't, then it would at least suffice for the world he was in.

They passed through a park, in the center of which stood a large building of black marble which Odd said was the building of civic administration. Thence through a district in which smart shops displayed their wares, and down a broad avenue lined with royal palms and faced on either side by magnificent estates. Odd explained that these were the homes of the more wealthy citizens of Karneter.

Presently, far down the avenue, Buell descried a beautiful building, Gothic in type, a mass of pointed towers, spires and minarets. In the distance the building looked blue. Buell first ascribed this to the effect of the intervening air or perhaps the reflection of the sky, but as he drew nearer he discovered that it actually was blue—a light robin's-egg shade, trimmed with ornaments of burnished gold.

At length they drew up before a golden gate, the high walls on each side of which also were blue.

"The Temple of Isis," announced Odd.

As they approached, Buell had noticed two tall guards before the gate. Now, to his surprize, he saw that they were women—and such women! Neither could have been less than six feet two inches in height, broad of shoulder, full-breasted, and with muscular arms and legs that would have made them formidable antagonists in the boxing ring or on the wrestling mat. They were armed, like the guards at the Temple of Re, with a spear and simitar apiece.

"The N would view the Temple of Isis ere he goes on his long journey," said Odd, addressing one of the Amazonian guards.

Leaning her tall spear against the wall, she unfastened the gate and swung it back. As they passed through, Buell noticed that she smiled archly up at his tall companion. It appeared that she was flirting with him, nor did her coyness seem out of place, for although she was a giantess to Buell, she appeared quite dainty and petite when compared to the huge Odd.

"I see that you have large women in Karneter as well as big men," remarked Buell.

"Not many," Odd replied. "About two hundred

of each. The women guard the Temple of Isis and the men the Temple of Osiris."

"I had no idea there were so many giants in the world," said Buell.

"Perhaps there are not in the upper world," his guide replied. "Our race began here with only a few which Mezzar Hashin the First brought with him from the upper world. But by eugenic marriages, eliminating all individuals who are undersized, we have grown quite rapidly in numbers, for giants. We are fed special rations to keep up our vitality, and in addition, have a medicine mixed with our food at certain intervals, that acts beneficially on our thyroid glands—the real cause of our superior size."

"I presume, then, that all of you are more or less related."

"That is true. The girls at the gate are both distant cousins of mine." He sighed. "I suppose that I shall have to marry one of them soon. I dislike the thought of matrimony, but we are only permitted the freedom of a single life up to the age of thirty, and I am now twenty-nine. If I do not choose a suitable mate before that time one will be chosen for me by the scientists."

"Are there many men as large as you?"

"None quite so large," was the reply. "That is why I was chosen for the post I now occupy. If one of the young men now growing up becomes larger than I his name will be Odd and he will take my place while I will become an officer of the Temple Guards."

As was the case with the Temple of Re, the grounds were beautifully landscaped with flowers, trees and shrubbery. Slaves clad in dark blue labored here as in the temple of the sun god, but all were women. Maidens, attired in clinging, light blue garments trimmed with gold, wandered about the grounds gathering flowers and fruits. These, Odd said, were the vestal virgins of Isis. Older and more matronly-appearing women, attired in heavier and stiffer garments of the same light shade of blue, but trimmed with silver, and with their heads shaven, so Odd informed Buell, were priestesses of Isis.

They drew near to the portal of the temple, and Buell saw that it was guarded by more giantesses, some of them fully seven feet in height. He also observed that tall Amazons were posted at intervals around the walls.

At the portico they paused a moment while Odd made known their intentions to the guard. An elderly priestess came out in a few moments and escorted them through the door.

The beauty and magnificence of the exterior of the building had given promise of a splendid interior, but Buell was hardly prepared for the dazzling glory of the huge auditorium in which he found himself. The vault of cerulean blue above his head formed the setting for thousands of tiny lights, each constantly appearing, disappearing and reappearing, as if a gigantic swarm of fireflies had been hovering there. Set in the gold-tinted walls were life-size paintings depicting the exploits of Isis as recorded in Egyptian mythology, showing her watering the crops of her worshipers, thus insuring them a bounteous harvest, and representing her as a giver of dreams, inflicter of diseases and restorer of health. As in the Temple of Re, statues of the lesser deities lined the walls. At the far end of the room, incense smoldered on an altar before a large golden throne set with precious stones and upholstered with blue velvet. On each side of this throne, huge statues, one of Anubis and the other of Horus, knelt as if in adoration or supplication.

Buell surveyed the scene with wonder and admiration. The elderly priestess, with a backward glance in his direction, left them in the middle of the floor.

"Look well on these splendors," admonished Odd. "You are being accorded a special privilege. Throughout the year no man is allowed to enter this temple or even the temple grounds under pain of death, at other than stated hours on the regular days of worship, except the High One. The N, however, is permitted a last look at its glories before entering the inner Karneter. The Odd, being his constant companion, must accompany him."

BUELL scarcely heard the rumbling voice, so engrossed was he by the sight of a figure that had come through a doorway at his right, the slight, shapely figure of a girl encased in a clinging filmy garment of light blue gossamer silk that harmonized with the blue of her eyes. The band of blue velvet that bound her fluffy hair held a glittering star in place above her forehead. She wore belt, sandals, breastplates and armlets of burnished gold. It was not these things, however, that held Buell's attention as he watched her coming toward him with her pudgy companion, a fat priestess who read aloud to her from a papyrus scroll, but the walk and appearance of the girl herself. Scarcely crediting the evidence of his senses, he waited until she drew closer. Then he knew!

"Doris!" he cried.

She turned, then with a little gasp of recognition ran into his arms.

"I knew you would come, Alan," she murmured, looking up with brimming eyes. "I have been so frightened and so—"

There was a bellowing roar from Odd.

"What sacrilege is this?"

Alan was jerked backward with such violence that he lost his balance and fell to the floor at the feet of the giant.

Buell saw red. Hot flames of anger scorched every fiber of his being as he heard Odd muttering something about the sacred person of Isis, Bride of Osiris. His hands encountered a slack coil of the heavy chain that bound him to the monster. Acting more through instinct than reason, he gathered it in both hands, leaped to his feet, and swung for the face of the giant. At the first blow Odd toppled like a great oak cut nearly through. As Buell swung the heavy chain once more, he fell with a crash.

There was a squeal of alarm and rage. Then someone leaped upon Buell's back, clawing at his face. It was the fat priestess.

Shaking her off, he dived for the belt pouch of the prostrate Odd, took a bunch of keys therefrom and rapidly tested them on the padlock that held the chain about his waist. At last he found the right one, turned the lock, and leaped free of his shackles.

Meanwhile the squealing priestess had alarmed the guards at the main door. Two of them came running toward him.

"Oh, Alan, they will kill you!" Doris Lee's eyes were wide with fear.

"Does this door lead into the garden?" he asked.

"Yes, but it is guarded."

"Come. It's our only chance. If we can win through to the wall I think I can get you out of here."

As they hurried through the narrow side entrance, their pursuers, now only a hundred feet behind them, set up a clamor that Buell felt sure would alarm the outer guards.

He was right. A giantess stood with feet braced at the doorway, her spear-point barring his progress. Doris screamed when he ran forward as if to throw himself on the keen point. Suddenly, just as he seemed about to be impaled, he swerved to one side, ran forward again, and dived. It was a brilliant flying tackle, the equal of any he had ever made in his football days. The giantess dropped her spear, clutched wildly at the doorway for support, and missing it, toppled and fell down the steps. Releasing his hold, Buell caught up the long spear, and taking Doris' hand, raced off with her through the shrubbery.

They followed a winding path for some distance unmolested. Then a garden slave, sensing the meaning of the uproar behind them, barred their progress for a moment. Buell presented his spear and the slave fled, panic-stricken. He smiled grimly as they ran forward again.

"I wouldn't have used it on a woman," he said, "but it sure had the desired effect. Hello! Here's the wall. We'll be out of here now in a jiffy."

The wall was fully fifteen feet in height, and made more formidable by a row of down-curved spikes that projected near the top. A low hedge about three feet wide and composed of exceedingly thorny shrubs further added to its inaccessibility.

Placing his foot on the spear-shaft just behind the head, Buell snapped off the keen point. Then, pausing but a moment to calculate the distance, he ran forward, planted the butt of the shaft on the ground, and vaulted for the summit. Alighting on the edge of the wall rather than the top, for the pole was a trifle shorter than the wall, he endeavored to twist his body over. He half succeeded in this, but the smooth top offered no hand-hold, and he fell back on the curved spikes. The fact that they were curved downward saved him from injury, and the spikes themselves saved him from falling among the thorny bushes below.

Quickly clambering to the top of the wall, he held the spear-shaft, which still leaned against the wall between two of the spikes, down to Doris.

"Take hold of this," he said, "and I'll pull you up."

"B-but the spikes," she quavered, "and those thorny bushes. I might fall."

"It is the only way. Be brave." She came forward and took hold of the shaft. Leaning far out, he swung her clear of the bushes. Then, just as he had drawn her half-way up the wall, a giantess darted from the shrubbery behind and seized her around the waist, pulling her from the shaft. Buell swung it back for a blow at her captor, when two huge hands seized his ankles from behind, tipping him over backward.

Two Amazonian guards, laughing exultantly, handed him down the human ladder which they had formed against the wall with the aid of seven of their companions.

CHAPTER 13
RAFFERTY LIMBERS HIS JOINTS

A LONE in the narrow, winding passageway, Dan Rafferty moved forward cautiously. Presently the rays from his pocket flashlight revealed the wrinkled, disfigured countenance of the prisoner who had begged for a word with him.

"Yez'll have to be brief," he said. "Me matey will be lookin' for me in a few minutes, and I don't want to be pinched just for the pleasure av listenin' to your blarney."

The shackled man stared up at him with a crafty look in his single, beady eye. The other—the one that had been gouged out—was closed in a ghastly wink.

"You wish to get out of Karneter, do you not?" he asked.

"Sure, and I would like nothin' better, provided two or three very good friends of mine could be included in the party.."

"Who are these friends?"

"Alan Buell, now called the Osiris N, whativver

that may be, and who I understand is to be kilt at the Festival of Re. Also his girl, Doris Lee. They say she's goin' to become Isis and marry that Hashish gink. Likewise a girl named Delra, who works in the Temple of Re — that is providin' she wants to go. I've made up me mind to ask her the first chance I get."

The prisoner stood suddenly erect. There was a quiet dignity in his manner as he replied.

"You are fortunate in having come to me, for I am the only man in Karneter who can and will help you, and that for a trifling service. Behold me, Alcibar, once High Priest of Re, and second in command in Karneter, reduced to this." For a moment his voice choked with emotion. Then he continued: "Wealth, luxury, pomp, position — all were mine. Then came the lies, foul slanderous lies, whispered in the ear of the High One by a man I had loved as a brother — a man I had advanced to the position next to mine. I was accused of plotting to overthrow Mezzar Hashin and establish myself as the Osiris. There was not a thread of truth in the accusations, but the High One — the Fiendish One, as I now know him to be — believed them, or pretended to do so. I was tortured, mutilated, maimed, but through it all I maintained my innocence. Then I was committed to this, the punishment of the lowest, the most debased criminals in Karneter. And Sethral, he who had betrayed my friendship, was made High

Priest of Re in my stead."

"Tough luck," commented Rafferty, "but get to the point. What do yez want me to do? Assassinate them two guys? And what do I get in return?"

"You have tools in that bag that will cut through this chain. Release me and I pledge you my word that I will get you and your friends out of Karneter. As for Sethral and Hashin, think you that I would permit anyone to cheat me of my vengeance? Both shall die by my hand and mine alone."

"Suits me," replied Dan, "if you're handin' me the straight dope, although I'd like wan good sock at that Hashin guy mesilf. Anyhow I'm willin' to take a chance. A slim chance is better than none at all."

He laid his tool kit on the floor and unbuckled the flap. The largest pair of nippers he had failed to more than nick the chain.

"Have to file it," he said. He straightened up suddenly, listening. "The divvil. No time for that either. I hear somebody comin'."

"Leave the file with me," whispered Alcibar as the sound of voices and footsteps grew louder. "You can say you lost it if you are questioned. I'll find a way to communicate with you as soon as I am free."

"All right, here goes."

Rafferty handed him the file, buckled the flap of his tool kit, and hurried off. Arriving at the six cor-

Otis Adelbert Kline

ners he saw lights and heard voices in the main passageway.

"Seboul," he called.

"Is that you, Baku?"

Two men were coming toward him: Seboul and one of the dungeon guards.

"Sure it's me. Where the divvil did yez go?"

"I missed you at the stairway. Then I searched, with the assistance of the guard."

"Guess I got mixed up," said Dan. "I walked past a lot of skeletons and a few corpses. Then, seein' you weren't wid me, I turned around and came back here."

"You did the right thing. We will go up now. Better keep close to me so we won't be separated again."

They made their way up the stairways and through the various passageways into the rear of the temple without further incident. They were met by the sour-faced priest who had guided them.

"You did a poor job on the image of Isis this morning," he grumbled. "None of the lights will work now. Why doesn't the Department send men who understand their business?"

"I had it workin' this morning," replied Rafferty. "Mebby somewan has jimmed up the works. Let's look it over, Seboul. You test the light bulbs and I'll check up on the switches."

"See that it works this time," warned the priest.

"If it doesn't I'll report you to the Department."

"Don't worry, Cap," responded Dan.. "When I get through wid it it'll work."

The surly priest left, muttering to himself, and the two men set to work.

As before, Dan investigated the switches and wires behind the image while Seboul tested the lights in front. The identical short that he had repaired that morning seemed to be causing the trouble. A spark had apparently burned through the coating of tape he had applied.

RAFFERTY spread the wires farther apart and applied a double thick coating. He was tightening the last screw in the wall plate when he heard a door open softly behind him. Quickly turning, he beheld Delra the vestal virgin. She was carrying the narrow, jewel-incrusted vase from which she had poured incense on the alter that morning.

Scarcely had she stepped through the doorway when a man, dressed in the uniform of a temple guard, came up behind her and seized her roughly by the arm.

"One minute, elusive one," he said. "Haven't you played with me long enough? I saved you from the unwelcome attentions of Jethlo, yet you spurn me. What further task would you have me perform that I may win your favor?"

Attempting to pull away, but failing in this, the

girl looked scornfully up at him.

"Save me from your own attentions, Sessed," she replied. "Release me now, or I shall scream."

The fellow laughed. Suddenly he clapped his huge hand over her mouth. The vase dropped to the floor and shattered, its fragments mingling with the finely powdered incense.

"Now scream—yell all you want to."

The presence of Dan Rafferty had not been noted by either the girl or man.. Stepping quietly up to Sessed, Rafferty tapped him on the shoulder.

"Come, now. Behave like a gintleman and let go av the little lady."

Sessed regarded him with a sneer.

"Attend to your own affairs, slave," he retorted.

"Faith, I'll attend to you first."

Rafferty swung straight for the point of the man's jaw. Had the blow landed it would undoubtedly have settled the dispute, but Sessed was a trained fighter. He leaped back just in time to avoid the heavy fist of the Irishman. Then he whipped out his simitar.

"Put down that meat-ax and fight like a man," jeered Rafferty.

The girl was tugging at his arm.

"Run," she cried. "Escape before it is too late."

The burly face of Sessed was twisted in a sneer.

"I do not fight with slaves," he said. "I merely kill them like mad dogs when they require killing.

Out of the way, girl."

He advanced threateningly, although Delra was still between them.

"Hiding behind a woman will not avail you. You are doomed."

"Who's hidin' behind a woman?" Rafferty pushed Delra gently to one side. "Cut ahead, you butcher."

Sessed raised his simitar. It was then that Rafferty leaped. Seizing the wrist of his assailant with his left hand he pushed it back and downward, locking his right arm about the fellow's head at the same time.

The heavy weapon clattered to the floor, but Sessed was far from beaten. With a grunt of pain he sank his teeth into Rafferty's shoulder. It was not until then that the Irishman exerted his full strength.

"Bite like the damned dog yez are," he said. "I'll soon put a stop to it."

A swift downward push of the twisted arm and it snapped — then hung limp and useless. The grip of the guard's jaws relaxed, and he attempted to back away. He was assisted in this by a swift uppercut that lifted him clear off the floor, then sent him crashing into a corner, where he lay very still.

Glowering down at his assailant, Dan felt a soft hand on his arm. The girl was looking up at him with an expression in which were mingled admiration and fear.

"You had best go at once," she said. "Someone may come at any moment. If you are discovered your death will be certain and horrible."

Dan placed his huge hand over the small one on his arm.

"And would that make any difference to yez?"

"I wouldn't want to see a fellow countryman suffer."

"A fellow countryman? Begorry, yez don't mane to tell me—?"

"That I'm Irish? Assuredly. I worked for a wealthy woman who became a follower of Mezzar Hashin. After attending his meetings for a year or so she sold all her property and came to Karneter, not knowing where or what Karneter was. I foolishly listened to her story of a hidden paradise and came with her. She died, poor soul, died of grief when she realized what she had done. At her death I was placed here. I understand that the period of service is one year. At the end of that time I become the property of Mezzar Hashin, or if he does not want me, one of his nobles. Yes, I'm Irish. My name is Mary Mooney. My father, Pat Mooney, was a patrolman on the north side."

"Pat Mooney! I know him well. And you're his daughter! Delra--Mary darlint! There's a chance that I can find a way out av here—I and me friends. I love you, acushla." His arms went about the slender figure. "Will yez come wid me, Mary Mooney, if I can find a way out?"

"Will I come? Oh, Dan!" The thrilling rapture of her kiss told him of her consent a thousand times more agreeably than mere words.

"Seize him, men!"

Dan's heart skipped a beat at this sudden interruption. He turned to face a wall of sharp-pointed spears in the hands of a dozen stalwart temple guards. It was obvious that resistance was useless, so he held out his wrists for the manacles which two men brought forward.

The sour-faced priest who had been his guide some time before was addressing another, evidently of considerable importance and rank, to judge from the richness of the decorations on his yellow robes and his high, jewel-encrusted head-dress, in the center of which blazed a burnished golden disk.

"I saw him fighting with Sessed, most holy Sethral," the informer was saying. "The girl was standing near by."

So this was Sethral, High Priest of Re. He had a thin, ratlike face and huge, projecting upper teeth that would not stay within the confines of his receding lips. Dan saw him bend over the fallen guard.

"It seems that Sessed has been badly used," he said. Then, after a moment's examination. "Quite brutally used, in fact. He is dead."

"Is he to be taken immediately before the High

One?" The sour-faced informer was speaking again.

"No. The High One is to be troubled with no more cases until after the Festival of Re, for which he is now preparing. Confine this murderer and desecrator in the fourth dungeon until such time as the mighty Osiris is ready to pass judgment on him."

"And the girl?"

"For the present, five lashes will suffice."

Helpless rage gave way to dark despair as Dan, some twenty minutes later, was chained to the wall in the deepest, filthiest dungeon in Karneter, and left in its black solitude.

CHAPTER 14
THE FESTIVAL OF RE

HALF dazed though he was by the sudden turn of events which had again separated him from Doris and placed him in the hands of the Amazonian guards of the Temple of Isis, Buell struggled desperately to escape. The fact that he could not bring himself to strike a woman, even though that woman was a giantess and a trained fighter, made his efforts futile, and he soon found himself spread-eagled on the ground with a heavy female seated on his legs and two others holding his arms.

The sound of a familiar rumbling voice was followed by the appearance of the huge, masked face of its owner looming above him. Two livid welts showed on the exposed part of Odd's forehead. His usual calm manner, however, had not changed.

"Fool!" was all he said. Stooping, he made the heavy chain fast once more around Buell's waist. Then, motioning for the giantesses to release him, he dragged him to his feet and led him away.

Buell felt sure he would be punished for his attempted escape, but when? How? They reached the inner chamber of the Temple of Osiris which they had left that morning, without a word passing between them. Odd sat down behind the table with the two red lamps, motioned Buell to a chair, and took up a roll of papyrus.

"Your lessons will now commence," he rumbled.

Buell spent the rest of the day learning rituals and incantations and practising certain maneuvers with which it was essential that the N should be familiar. In fact, all his time up to the night before the Festival of Re was taken up in this manner, with the exception of a short walk, morning and evening, in the garden, mealtime, and the six hours that were permitted him at night for sleep. All this time he was chained to Odd, not even being allowed to remove his clothing at night.

It seemed to Buell that they retired much earlier than usual on the night before the festival, though he had no means of making certain. He noticed, too, that a feeling of extreme drowsiness crept over him as soon as he stretched himself on his cot—something that had not happened before. "Perhaps they have doped me," he thought, but his eyes closed languorously, heavily, and deep sleep temporarily shut out further worries.

His awakening was gradual and quite pleasant. He thought at first he was dreaming, as the sounds of soft, sweet music slowly penetrated his consciousness. As he lay there with eyes closed, his other senses gathered impressions. It seemed that the cot had been transformed to a downy bed with soft, silken coverlets. Instead of the damp smell of the inner chambers of the temple, he breathed sweet, pure air, laden with the delicate fragrance of jasmine, and tinged with a hint of musk and sandalwood.

Presently the music grew louder and he opened his eyes. The sense of sight confirmed the evidence of his other senses and added to it. He was indeed lying in a soft bed, a most luxurious bed with a scarlet canopy and silken coverlets, in a large room that was gorgeously decorated and lavishly furnished. The scent of jasmine came through a latticed window at his left—the music and faint odors of musk and sandalwood from a bevy of Oriental dancing girls who swayed in rhythmic unity as they played their stringed instruments just beyond the foot of his bed. Seeing him awake, they quickly withdrew, the music dying out as the last girl tripped through the door.

Then he noticed, for the first time, that he was attired in a soft, silken sleeping garment. The chain was no longer about his waist, nor was the giant, Odd, in sight.

A soft-footed servant approached his bed, salaamed thrice, and said: "Your bath is prepared, mighty Osiris."

The title of Osiris meant that Buell's day of doom had arrived. Somehow, sometime, during that day it was the intention of the powers of Karneter that he meet his death. As he had been taught certain rituals and incantations he might reasonably expect that the ceremonies in which they were to be used would all be enacted before the blow fell. On the other hand, it might be that they had taught him some things that he could not use in order that he might be thrown off his guard when the fatal moment arrived. If anything was to be done about saving Doris and himself it must be done quickly. He must be ever on his guard, yet seemingly resigned to his fate.

Leaping out of bed with assumed cheerfulness, he bathed luxuriously. After a brisk rub-down he donned the garments brought by the servant, rich garments of white silk, similar in every respect to those which had been worn by Mezzar Hashin in the Hall of the Two Truths. The headpiece, however, had a black "N" inscribed on the burnished disk that blazed above the center of the forehead.

Another servant, entering the. doorway, salaamed thrice as had the first, and announced that breakfast was served. Following the man to a magnificent dining room, he breakfasted in state, served by beautiful slave girls who pressed all manner of dainties on him.

After breakfast a servant brought him a black

mask that completely covered his face, a short, heavy shepherd's crook, and a three-lashed whip. Masked, and holding the crook and whip crossed over his breast after the manner of Osiris, he left the building and mounted to the cushioned seat of a golden litter with a scarlet canopy, borne by twelve of the scarlet-robed priests of Osiris.

The giant temple guards salaamed respectfully as he was carried out the gate. A row of them fell in line on each side of the litter and over at the left he could see lines of priests, vestal virgins and more temple guards forming.

Somewhere back in the procession a band of musicians struck up the strains of a marching song—a weird, shrieking blare of sound, rhythmic as the measured steps and chanting voices of the marchers, yet discordant if judged by modern standards.

Lining the streets in multi-hued holiday attire, the populace did homage to the Osiris N, making obeisance as the litter passed them. As they progressed the crowds grew thicker until the giant guards were compelled to push them back to let the procession through.

At the gate of the Temple of Re, where the crowd was thickest, the procession paused. The huge commander of the guards of Osiris was greeted by the commander of the guards of Re. The noise of the musicians ceased. Buell saw a fleet-footed messenger, dispatched by the latter commander, run to the portal of the temple. Scarcely had he entered it ere the distant beating of a giant drum sounded— throbbing, pulsating, thunderous in volume. The gates were flung wide and Buell was again carried forward by the scarlet-robed priests.

GARBED in the bridal robes of Isis, Doris Lee sat beneath the pale blue canopy of her palanquin in the Temple of Re, surrounded by her vestal virgins, her priestesses and her giant Amazonian guards. After her attempted escape from the Temple of Isis and her subsequent recapture she had expected punishment of some sort, but the pale blue lines beneath her eyes—the unwonted whiteness of her cheeks, had not been due to this cause alone, but rather to the fear that some dire punishment would be visited on Buell—that he would not be permitted to live even to the day on which Mezzar Hashin had previously decreed that he should die.

As no punishment had been visited on her she concluded that the person of Isis was held sacred, and fervently hoped that this might also be true in the case of the Osiris N. She had, however, prepared for emergency on the day before. While walking through the armory of her temple with her pudgy instructress she had managed to snatch unseen a slender dagger from a pile that lay on one of the tables. With the resolve that its keen blade should pierce her heart ere Mezzar Hashin could claim her for his own, she had concealed it beneath her garments and calmly entered the palanquin in which she was borne, at the head of her retinue, to the Temple of Re.

The multicolored footlights of the colossal image of Isis at the left of the altar had flashed on as she was carried through the portal of the temple, the walls of which were lined with spectators, representing, for the most part, the wealth and nobility of Karneter. Past these she was borne, to a position directly in front of the brilliantly lighted image of the goddess she now represented. The equally huge image of Osiris at the other side of the altar remained dark, and a space in front of it as large as that occupied by her own retinue was empty of people.

Directly in front of the altar crouched the yellow-robed priests of Re, their hands clasped in supplication, their faces toward the great blazing disk above it. Sethral, the High Priest, strode back and forth before the altar, muttering incantations as he walked and flinging a handful of incense from the jeweled vase he carried on the smoldering altar-fire each time he passed it.

The drowsy mumbling of the High Priest was suddenly interrupted by the clear voice of a runner who dashed through the doorway at the far end of the room.

"The Osiris N comes!" he shouted. "Prepare to

greet the Osiris N."

The heart of Doris Lee leaped to her throat as she grasped the significance of his words. Alan was alive! He was coming to the temple! There was yet hope!

Far above her head in the central dome of the temple she heard the sudden rumble of the huge drum as it roared the welcome of the mighty sun god to the Osiris N. There ensued a period of watching, during which no sound was heard save the throbbing of the great drum. Then she saw an erect, white-clad figure borne through the doorway on a golden litter carried by scarlet-robed priests. At the same moment the footlights illuminated the co-lossus of Osiris which stood at the right of the altar, and the spectators—even her own retinue, the yel-low-clad priests of Re, and the High Priest him-self—salaamed three times before the oncoming fig-ure.

Could it be that this was really Alan? Grave doubts assailed her. Would these nobles, even Sethral, second in command in Karneter, bow thus before a prisoner—a man condemned to death?

The mask hid his features, but as he drew closer she plainly made out the black "N" on the disk that fronted his headpiece—the mark which her instruc-tress had assured her would constitute the only dif-ference between his costume and that of Mezzar Hashin. As he took up his position before the image of Osiris, surrounded by his priests and vestal virgins and flanked by his gigantic guards, the beating of the great drum ceased, and was replaced by a burst of plaintive Oriental music.

Then, from the doorway at the left of the altar, came a troupe of dancing girls, vestal virgins of Re. As they danced before the palanquin of the Osiris N, Doris noticed that the back of one girl, more beautiful and graceful than the others, was covered with red welts on which blood had dried and caked.

The dance over, the girls withdrew and the music changed to a funeral dirge in which the voices of the yellow-robed priests joined.

The palanquin of the Osiris N was lowered and he stepped majestically to the floor, then walked to a place directly in front of the blazing image of the sun god. There followed a long ritual in which he took an active part, and during which Sethral, the High Priest, disappeared through a door at the right of the altar. The priests departed, one by one, until the Osiris N was left alone. After a few incantations he walked to the left of the altar. Scarcely had he taken his position there, when the Osiris, wearing a black mask, appeared as if by magic directly opposite him. The Osiris made a series of mystic passes which were faithfully duplicated by the Osiris N as by a mirror. It was then that Doris noticed that the Osiris hell his crook in his right hand and his whip in his left, while the Osiris N help the whip in the right hand and the crook in the left.

Suddenly the High Priest reappeared, wearing a hideous crocodile mask. In this character he was no longer Sethral, High Priest of Re, but Set, the crocodile god, mortal enemy of Osiris. Snapping the teeth of his mask, he advanced threateningly toward the two men, who drew close together as if for mutual protection. Then, with teeth still clashing, he rushed up the steps at the right of the altar and disappeared.

Still timing their movements in perfect unison, the Osiris and the Osiris N deposited their whips and crooks before the altar. A moment later, side by side, they mounted the steps up which the High Priest had gone and were also lost to view.

Doris turned to her instructress.

"Where have they gone, Thansor?" she asked.

"Into the most holy place, there to kneel with their backs to the golden disk in order that they may receive the *Sa*, the divine blessing of Re. "

"Then what will they do?"

"Have patience, glorious Isis, and you shall soon see for yourself."

For several moments following, all was still as death. It seemed that the entire audience had stopped breathing, waiting for and expecting something to happen.

Suddenly, from the hidden room, there came the sound of a muffled blow. Then there fluttered out from behind the disk a curious thing—a hideous, unbelievable thing. Doris watched it, fascinated with horror—a huge bird with body, wings and claws like that of an owl, but with the head of a man! The features, pale and deathlike, were the features of Alan Buell, and they were twisted in a horrid grin as they looked down at the half-fainting girl. It hovered aimlessly for a moment above the altar, then circled, and flying directly upward, disappeared through one of the ventilators. As it disappeared, the image of Osiris was darkened.

Eyes wide with terror, Doris seized the arm of her instructress.

"Thansor, tell me quickly, what was that?"

"That," replied Thansor with a hint of exultation in her voice, "was the *Ba*—the soul of the Osiris N."

CHAPTER 15
BEHIND THE SCENES

IN THE inky solitude of the deepest dungeon, Dan Rafferty, his feet braced against the slimy wall, was trying, as he had tried times without end, to break the heavy chain that held him. As day and night were alike to him and sleep came only with utter exhaustion, he had no idea how long he had been confined there. A few days, a week perhaps, but it seemed an age. True, an attendant had brought him food from time to time, but whether one, two or three meals a day, he had no means of knowing, for he was always hungry.

As he struggled grimly at his hopeless task the sound of a human voice, the first he had heard since his incarceration, came eerily to him from the darkness at his back. Someone was softly calling his name. Startled, he ceased his efforts and dropped, catlike, to his feet, turning as he dropped.

Again the unseen presence addressed him.

"Is that you, Dan Rafferty?"

"Sure, it's nobody else. And who the divvil may you be?"

"Hush! Not so loud!" He heard the unseen owner of the voice move stealthily closer. "I am Alcibar, the prisoner you befriended three days ago. Ever since I slipped my metal collar, thanks to your sharp file, I have been searching for you. Only today did I learn that you were confined here, so I have hastened to keep my promise."

"Did yez bring the file?"

"I did. Here, let me cut your collar for you. I believe that practise has made me quite adept."

Crouching there in the darkness, Dan waited stoically while the hard tool, stroke by stroke, cut into the metal that held him, nor did he more than wince on those occasions when it slipped and mingled his blood with the bits of metal that were falling on his neck.

After fully an hour of patient labor on the part of Alcibar and heroic endurance on the part of Rafferty, the stubborn metal yielded and Dan stood up. He shook himself like a beast of burden just freed from the yoke.

"Begorry, it feels good to have that damned thing off," he said, "even though most of me skin went with it. Where do we go from here?"

"We must make haste," replied Alcibar, "but we must also be cautious. First, remove your clothing. I have brought apparel more suitable than that you are wearing, for the work that lies before us."

Quickly slipping out of his slave garments, the

Irishman donned the new clothing which Alcibar provided.

"They are the robes of a priest of Re," he explained. "I am similarly attired and have gone about the temple all day undetected, so they should prove an excellent disguise for you."

"Righto," said Dan. "Let's go. Do yez know where we can find me friend Buell?"

"If I mistake not, he is now on his way to the temple, where he will shortly re-enact the story of the death of Osiris."

"Yez mane he's going to be kilt?"

"Precisely. We go now to save him. Re grant that we will be in time! Here, give me your hand."

Guided by Alcibar, Dan hurried through numerous passageways and corridors. The ex-priest, it seemed, had an almost uncanny knowledge of every twist and turn and a marvelous sense of direction. Presently they mounted a dark stairway, then another, faintly lighted, and still another in which they could see quite plainly.

"Pull your cowl over your head," admonished Alcibar. "We will have to pass many guards now, and the way is better lighted farther on."

They encountered two guards at the foot of the next stairway and passed them unchallenged. More guards and several priests were met and passed on the next level with the same result.

At the second basement level, the fifth above the

dungeon from which they had come, Rafferty's companion led him away from a stairway and through a gigantic storeroom piled with boxes, bales and casks.

"Our progress from now on," he said, "will be through a secret way known only to Mezzar Hashin, Sethral and myself. It is intended solely for the use of the Osiris and the High Priest of Re."

Walking behind a pile of boxes he stepped before a blank wall, apparently of solid masonry, reached upward to a chink above his head, inserted his finger and pushed. To the astonishment of Rafferty, a cunningly concealed door, made of metal and faced with stone that exactly matched the stone around it, swung open. Behind it was a spiral, metal stairway.

The two men entered the aperture. Then Alcibar pulled the door shut after him and led the way up the steps.

AFTER climbing for some distance they arrived at a square landing, from which two narrow passageways branched in opposite directions. Hearing footsteps above him, Dan judged that they were just beneath one of the floors of the temple. They took the passageway which led to the right and, following it for some distance, arrived at the foot of a short, straight stairway.

Turning, the ex-priest placed his hand on Dan 's arm.

"From now on," he said, "we must preserve absolute quiet. The slightest sound may mean sudden death for both of us."

He mounted the steps with catlike tread and Dan followed, scarcely permitting himself to breathe. At the top, Alcibar cautiously raised a trap-door and peered through the orifice. Then he pushed it up silently and stepped to the floor above, beckoning Rafferty to follow. They were in a narrow, dimly lighted space between a paneled wall and a thick, yellow curtain.

Alcibar lowered the trap-door once more, tiptoed to the end of the curtain, and peered around it.

"All is well so far," he whispered.

He next applied his single eye to a tiny hole in the paneled wall. "Come," he said. "I will show you one of your friends."

Dan looked through the hole. A semicircle of yellow-robed priests knelt before the altar, which was slightly to the left of his line of vision, while Sethral walked back and forth before it, muttering incantations and throwing incense in the flames. At his right he saw the huge image of Isis, the lighting switches of which he had twice repaired. A priest of Re was operating them. In the hall beyond he saw a vast crowd of people, and quite near him a beautiful girl in a blue-canopied litter, surrounded by blue-garbed virgins, priestesses and giant Amazonian guards.

"Don't see anybody I know," he said.

"The girl beneath the blue canopy. Do you not know her? She is the fiancée of your friend, Alan Buell."

"Begorry, is that Doris Lee? Sure and the bye picked himself a peach! If I'd nivver seen Mary Mooney I'd call her the prettiest girl I ivver clapped eyes on."

As Dan turned away from the opening a hollow, rhythmic booming sounded above their heads.

"Your friend has arrived at the temple gates," said Alcibar. "The great drum beats the welcome of Re to the Osiris N."

While Alcibar talked he lifted the lid of a huge, gilded chest that stood in one corner, searched among its contents for a moment, and then drew forth a gaudy yellow robe similar to that worn by the High Priest. Removing his plain robe, he donned it. From another section of the chest he took two weapons that made Dan Rafferty dance with delight. They were short clubs, each weighted at one end with a ball of iron the size of a lemon and ringed with a leather wrist-loop at the other end.

"Faith, that's a pretty pair of shillalahs," said Dan.

Alcibar flung his old robe into the chest and closed the lid. Then he handed one of the clubs to Dan.

The beating of the great drum was suddenly

stilled, and the plaintive strains of Oriental music burst forth from somewhere behind them.

"The dance begins," said Alcibar. "If you will look out the spy-hole you may be able to see Delra."

Dan looked.

"The dirty divvils!" he exclaimed. "Oh, the dirty, cowardly divvils! Would yez look at that poor little white back all covered with bloody welts. If I ivver get me two hands on that High Priest I'll—"

"Stop!" The single eye of the former High Priest regarded him sternly. "Remember, when the time comes, the life of Sethral belongs to me. It is I who have suffered most at his hands."

"In that case," replied Dan, "here's wishin' yez luck, and I hope yez break ivvery bone in his body."

"If things work out as planned I can at least guarantee that he will never see the light of another day. Better let me at the spy-hole now. It will soon be time for our part in the ceremony."

Chafing with impatience, Dan leaned against the paneled wall while his companion kept watch. Presently the music changed.

"Is Mary—I mane Delra, out there yet?"

"No, she has gone with the rest of the dancers, but have no fear. I will know where to find her when the time comes."

Rafferty fidgeted uneasily as he stood listening to the sounds from without. This waiting jarred on his nerves. Here he was, a fighting, two-fisted Irishman with a perfectly good club in his hands, and only a few feet from him were a score of polls he would dearly love to crack. He took a turn up and down the narrow space, hefting the weapon, testing its balance, and swinging, now and then, at an imaginary enemy. Tiring of this amusement at length, he stopped and peered around the heavy yellow curtain. Beyond it he saw a small, empty room, across the opposite side of which was stretched another similar curtain. A door in the wall at his right was closed.

Presently an odd, clattering noise came from the direction of the altar. Alcibar bounded noiselessly past him and crouched beside the door, his club gripped in his right hand.

"Get behind the curtain," he said, "and make not the slightest sound or movement until I call to you. The time for action has come."

CHAPTER 16
THE BRIDE OF OSIRIS

WHEN Doris Lee saw the unearthly thing that fluttered upward from the room which Buell had entered, she did not, of course, give credence to the statement of the fat priestess that it was the soul of Alan Buell. She believed that the vaunted magic of the Egyptian priests was legerdemain, pure and simple, even though they sometimes appeared to work miracles. What she really feared was that the harpylike creature symbolized the flight of his soul—in short, that he had really been slain. Her hand stole to the keen dagger beneath her girdle and rested there uncertainly for a moment. No. She would wait. She must make sure that all hope was lost before plunging alone into the great, dark beyond.

With fear-filled eyes she watched the preparations for the next part of the ceremony. A group of soldiers in suits and helmets of crocodile leather rushed in through a side door in disorderly array, shouting hoarsely and waving their simitars aloft. Her instructress had taught her to know the various masks, uniforms and insignia, and she recognized them as followers of Set, the crocodile god, mortal enemy of Osiris. Ten of their number carried a crucible of molten lead with charcoal blazing beneath it. Six more bore a huge gilded chest of strange design. On each side were four planes, slanting upward toward the front. A small propeller and rudder were attached to the rear.

The crucible was placed before the altar. The chest was laid directly in front of it. Still shouting and brandishing their weapons, the leather-clad soldiers danced about it.

A flash of yellow at the right of the altar caught her eye. It was the High Priest, still wearing the crocodile mask and gnashing the teeth as he moved the hideous muzzle from side to side. Behind him he dragged a limp, white-clad form.

At sight of the priest the soldiers redoubled their cries and several of their number rushed up the steps to meet him. They picked up the white-clad body and carried it toward the chest while two of their comrades removed the massive lid.

Was it the body of Buell? The features were still covered with the black mask, but she strove for a view of the disk that fronted the head-piece. As four men raised the body, preparatory to placing it in the chest, the head fell back and she saw a black "N" standing out boldly on the disk. The dancing figures swam mistily before her eyes. She tried to pluck the dagger from her girdle, but, weakened and half fainting as she was, she was scarcely able to move her hand. She must wait—wait until strength returned.

When her vision cleared once more the followers of Set were fastening the lid and sealing it with the molten lead. This task completed, they swung the chest to their shoulders and, led by the High Priest, carried it out of the room, still shouting and brandishing their weapons. A group of temple slaves removed the sizzling crucible.

Thansor, her fat instructress, looked up with a gloating expression on her moonlike face.

"The chest will now be shot into the lake," she said, "symbolizing the hurling of the chest containing the body of Osiris into the Nile after Set and his followers had betrayed him."

Too numb with horror to reply, Doris leaned back in her palanquin with half-closed eyes and prayed for strength.

When the last leather-clad figure had disappeared through the doorway, the followers of Osiris set up an unearthly wailing that was joined in by her own women. The moon-faced priestess again addressed Doris.

"Weep," she said. "Weep for the departed Osiris N. It is in the ritual that Isis should so weep."

Doris looked down at her dully. "I can not," she replied, and turned her head away.

The cries of the mourners were interrupted by a shout from behind her palanquin. Then, hurtling past her she saw the hawk-masked Horus. At his heels a horde of men in jackets that bristled with hawk feathers followed, shouting: "Where is Set? Where is the cowardly assassin of our lord, Osiris?"

"Who seeks Set?" The High Priest, still wearing the crocodile mask, appeared in the doorway and advanced threateningly, followed by the leather-clad soldiers.

"Horus, son of Osiris. Horus, the avenger, seeks the slayer of his father."

There followed a realistic sham battle between the followers of Set and those of Horus. Presently the leather-clad men were put to flight and the High Priest was brought, manacled, before the palanquin of Isis.

It was here that Doris' part in the ritual commenced, but she sat, gazing dully at the prisoner until the fat priestess prompted her. Then she repeated the lines automatically, like one in a dream.

"Unlock the fetters," whispered the priestess, handing her a key.

Like a person in a trance, she rose, stepped down from the palanquin, and released the High Priest. Things took the semblance of a vivid, terrifying dream. She saw Horus, shouting—gnashing his great hawk bill as if enraged by her action. Then he rushed up to her, tore the diadem from her head, and hurled it to the floor.

From behind her now came Thoth of the ibis mask. In his hands he carried a mask shaped like a cow's head—the mask of the cow goddess, Athor. Doris' knees were trembling weakly as he slipped the thing over her head.

Through the slits in the stuffy mask she saw the High Priest run up the steps to the right of the altar and disappear. The thunderous voice of the great temple drum resounded through the place, and again the lights flashed on the giant image of Osiris. A deafening shout went up from the multitude.

"Welcome, O son of Re! Thrice welcome, mighty Osiris, Lord of Karneter!"

All about her, people were prostrating themselves, their faces toward the altar. Then she saw a figure, clad in the white garments of Osiris, descending the steps. Instead of a black mask and diadem, the shoulders were crowned with the horned mask of the bull, Apis.

The figure advanced toward her, reached for a hand and clasped hers. Came a shout from the kneeling multitude.

"Hail to Isis, Bride of Osiris and co-ruler of Karneter!"

At the shock of these words she awakened as from a dream. Strength came to her—the strength of desperation. Wrenching her hand free, she tore the keen dagger from her girdle and plunged it into her bosom.

CHAPTER 17
IN THE MOST HOLY PLACE

ALTHOUGH Buell appeared passive to the onlookers as he went through his part of the ritual, observing every detail with the utmost nicety, his nerves were taut as bowstrings, his every faculty alert. At some point in the ceremonies lurked death, waiting to leap out at him — carry him into the black void of eternity. For Doris' sake as well as for his own, he must be ready to avoid the hand of the grim reaper until he had accomplished his purpose — the death of Mezzar Hashin.

As he stood before the altar, mirroring the motions of Hashin in accordance with the teachings of Odd, he tried to devise a way to end the life of his enemy. He thought of the crook, but no. It was too light. It might stun yet not kill. He would leap forward and throttle him. But again, no. It took time to throttle a man, and the guards would be upon him in an instant.

They mounted the steps at the right of the altar and entered a room across two ends of which were stretched heavy yellow curtains. The High Priest, still wearing the crocodile mask, awaited them. This was better. Here there would be but two men to fight. Outside there were thousands. The High Priest spoke.

"The Osiris and the Osiris N will kneel with their backs to the blazing disk that they may receive the *Sa*, the divine blessing of Re."

Both men knelt with their backs to the priest. As he bent forward, Buell twisted his black mask slightly to the right, that he might watch the movements of the priest, for he had seen his hand steal beneath his robe. Perhaps it concealed a deadly weapon.

As he watched from the corner of his eye his suspicions were confirmed, for the High Priest, while mumbling some incoherent incantations, drew an iron-headed mace from beneath his yellow robe and raised it to strike. When the blow fell he threw himself to one side, then leaped to his feet and swung for where he judged the priest's jaw to be beneath the crocodile mask.

To his intense surprize a powerful hand reached out from behind the curtain and caught his arm, checking the blow and whirling him about. The owner of the hand spoke softly.

"Not so fast, me bye. Not so fast. Would yez punch a friend in the face?"

"Dan Rafferty!" he exclaimed. "How in blazes

did you get here?"

"Shush. Not so loud. Yez'll have the army down on us like a swarm av bees. Now that Hashin's dead—"

"What?"

He turned and saw, for the first time, that the blow had fallen on the head of Mezzar Hashin, who was sprawled on the floor with a tiny stream of blood trickling from the back of his head. The priest had dragged something from beyond the farther curtain. It was a cage in which a great horned owl sat, blinking in the unaccustomed glare of light.

Opening the door of the cage, the priest removed the bird, avoided a vicious peck from its sharp, curved beak, and quickly slipped a mask over its head, fastening it with tough strands of thin, barely visible thread, which he wound about the body just beneath the wings. With a start of surprize, Buell saw that the mask was a hideously contorted likeness of his own face.

The mask in place, the priest pulled a cord that opened a panel in the ceiling of the small room, and tossed the bird up through it.

Rafferty caught at his sleeve and took the arm of Alan.

"Buell," he said, "I want you to meet up wid me friend, Alcibar. Alcie, shake hands wid Mr. Buell. Take off yer masks so yez'll know what each other looks like."

The former High Priest removed his mask, and Buell his. They shook hands gravely. Buell scanned the hideous, mutilated features.

"I should rather meet you any day than Sethral," he said.

"Sethral will never slay another Osiris N," replied Alcibar. "Behold."

He lifted the yellow curtain. The body of the High Priest of Re was huddled on the floor behind it. A bloody dent in the right temple showed how he had died.

"Alcie croaked him as soon as he stuck his head in the door," said Dan. "It was wan peach of a wallop."

The ex-priest dropped the curtain. "We must go on with the ceremony," he said. "If there is a break, someone may suspect that all is not well. Here, help me with this carcass."

From a pocket of his gown he took tape and gauze, with which he bound the bleeding wound in the head of Hashin, while Rafferty held it up. Then, taking Buell's mask and head-dress, he placed them on the head of the corpse, donned his own mask, and dragged the body from the room.

"A slick bye, Alcie," said Dan when he was gone. "Used to be High Priest himself. Knows all the ropes."

"He isn't much for looks," replied Buell, "but he seems to be a square shooter."

"It was Hashin spoiled his looks and Sethral put him up to it," explained Dan. "That's how it happens that he's on our side. They did him dirt and they've paid the penalty, but he ain't through yet. He told me there's several more lubbers he wants to get before he checks out. Says he's livin' only for revenge, but he'll help us get out of this place before he settles wid the other bozos."

"That's generous of him," answered Buell.

"It ain't so much generosity. He made a bargain wid me, and he's a man of his word. I got him out of the dungeon. Now he's going to try to get us out of Karneter."

He drew back the yellow curtain and stepped behind it. Presently he called softly to Buell.

"Come here, lad," he said, "and take a peek at the grand funeral they're givin' for yez."

Peering through the spy-hole, Buell saw the leather-clad soldiers place the body of Hashin in the chest, nail down the lid, and seal it with molten lead. He turned his gaze in the direction of Doris and noticed that her hand stole toward her girdle, then dropped listlessly. How pale she looked, and how utterly forlorn! If only he might reveal the truth to her! But there was no way. The ceremony must be concluded.

He and Rafferty took turns watching the battle between the followers of Set and those of Horus, and the ceremonies that followed. Shortly after his fetters had been unlocked by Doris, Alcibar rushed into the room. Flinging back the lid of the gilded chest in the corner, he took therefrom a mask like the shaggy head of a bull.

"You are now to wear this mask of the bull, Apis," he said. "Stand on the topmost step until the people have welcomed you. Then walk down and take the hand of Isis. Stand with her until they have proclaimed her the Bride of Osiris. At that point you are supposed to unmask. To do so, however, would be fatal, as the people would tear you, limb from limb. Instead you must lead her back up the steps as quickly as possible. It may be that I can then find a way of escape for you."

Straightening his heavy bull mask, Buell stepped out in full view of the people. Pausing for a moment to receive their adulation, he advanced to where Doris stood and took her hand. At the words: "Hail to Isis, Bride of Osiris and co-ruler of Karneter," he started to lead her back toward the altar in accordance with their prearranged plan. It was then that she twisted her hand free, whipped out the dagger and plunged it into her breast. He leaped forward, caught her wrist in a grip of steel, and forced it back, but the point of the dagger was wet with her blood. She slumped limply into his arms.

With an agonized cry, he tore the mask of Athor from her head. Her eyes were closed, her nostrils moving slightly. A mixed crowd had gathered closely around them. Thoth and Horus drove them back.

"Doris," he cried, "it is I, Alan, come to save you."

She opened her eyes slowly—looked up at the ugly bull mask.

"Lies!" she said. "Lies! Lies!"

Thoth, however, was not so incredulous. He knew the sound of Hashin's voice so well that Alan's first word had aroused his suspicion. Stepping quickly behind him, he jerked off the mask of Apis.

"A usurper!" he shouted. "It is the Osiris N! Slay him!"

Instantly Buell faced a ring of bared simitars and couched spears. Horus whipped out his keen blade and presented it at Buell's heart.

"Surrender!" he rasped. "Surrender or die!"

CHAPTER 18
THE VENGEANCE OF ALCIBAR

AS HE stood there in the midst of the hostile multitude holding the half-fainting Doris and expecting instant death, Buell heard two sounds simultaneously — the twang of a bow-string and an encouraging shout from Rafferty.

Horus, with an arrow through his throat, uttered a choking cry and slumped forward. Buell wrenched the simitar from his death-grip and, supporting Doris with his left arm, laid about him with the keen weapon. The crowd drew back a little at his furious onslaught. Then a giant form bore down on him — the huge commander of the guards of Osiris. He swung his six-foot simitar in a blow that would have sheared off Buell's head as easily as a blade of grass. Alan ducked, leaped forward, and ran him through the middle. As he crashed back on those behind him, Buell caught a glimpse of two figures behind the altar. A vestal virgin and a yel-low-robed priest were firing arrows into the crowd as fast as they could fit them to the bowstrings. An-other figure, also attired as a priest of Re, was smashing through the crowd toward him, cracking heads and arms to right and left as he swung two heavy maces with flail-like blows.

In another instant Buell and Rafferty were fighting, side by side with Doris between them, supported by the arm of the former.

The arrows continued to take deadly toll of those around them as they backed toward the altar. Time and again the lives of one or the other were saved by the swift shafts of Delra or Alcibar, who had turned the toy weapons of the vestal virgins to good advantage.

At length they made the steps. Here Buell and Rafferty held the crowd at bay while Delra helped Doris to the temporary safety of the Holy Place.

Alcibar, his arrows gone, seized the brazier of burning incense and hurled it in the faces of the attackers, momentarily blinding those who stood in front.

"Come quickly," he called. "Follow me."

As they ran into the room behind the blazing disk, several heavy spears struck around them. Alcibar slammed the door and slid the bolt in place. Delra was binding the wound in Doris' breast, a wound that was not deep because of the quick intervention of Buell.

Raising the heavy curtain, the ex-priest opened the trap-door behind it.

"Down the steps, all of you!" he cried. "There is

not a moment to lose. The soldiers may be deterred for a time by fear of the Holy Place, but it will not be for long."

Securing his simitar to his wrist by its tasseled cord, Buell helped Doris down the steps. Rafferty followed with Delra, and Alcibar came after them, pausing only to close and bolt the trap-door. He called to Buell.

"Turn to the left. I will lead the way in a moment"

They hurried down the dimly lighted passageway as directed. Presently Alcibar caught up with them, then took the lead.

"We are now beneath the temple gardens," he said. "From here we pass directly under the city."

They pressed forward in silence. Buell's numerous wounds, unnoticed until now in the heat of battle, smarted painfully. His once beautiful silk costume hung on him in shreds. Alcibar had apparently come through unscathed, though his magnificent robes were bedraggled and there was a bloodstain on his sleeve. Doris' self-inflicted wound had left a crimson stain on the breast of her pale blue garment. Like Alcibar, Delra was unwounded in the recent encounter, but her scant dancing costume revealed the welts she had received from the whip, some of which had been reopened by her exertions. Swinging along beside her with her slender arm in his huge left hand and the two maces dangling from his right, Dan Rafferty proudly carried the marks of battle. His yellow robe was full of rents and covered with bloodstains, and the cowl had been completely torn away. A simitar-cut above his left eyebrow gave him a rather ferocious expression. When they had traveled for a considerable distance he called to Alcibar.

"Where the divvil is that boat yez were tellin' me about, Alcie? Is it in Port Said or Honolulu?"

"About a half-mile farther on. We should be there in a few minutes."

Faintly at first, but gradually growing more distinct, came the sound of voices and footsteps in the passageway behind them.

"They're coming," called Buell. "Hurry ahead, all of you. I'll be the rear-guard."

"Now be the bones of St. Patrick's toe, where do yez get that stuff?" replied Rafferty indignantly. "I'll be the rear-guard."

"No time for argument. We'll guard the rear together. The girls can go forward with Alcibar."

Buell clutched his simitar, Rafferty took a mace in each hand, and they fell back about fifty feet behind the others. The expected attack came a few minutes later. Fortunately for the pursued, the pursuers were the giant guards of Osiris, who fought at a disadvantage in the low, narrow passageway, as they could only come forward one at a time and all had to stoop to avoid the arched ceiling.

Rafferty beat down the guard of the first man with a mace and Buell thrust him through the throat. The next man fought more warily, but finally succumbed to a blow from an iron shillalah, falling across the body of his companion. The third guard carried a spear. He made a lunge at Rafferty, but the Irishman seized the weapon and jerked him forward so that he stumbled across the bodies of the other two. Again Buell's simitar drank blood.

"Come on," said Dan. "They'll have to pull thim three hulks out av the way before they can get through now."

They hurried forward once more and presently saw Alcibar and the two girls waiting for them.

"Go on. What're yez waitin' for?" asked Dan.

"We're waiting for you," replied Alcibar. "I now have a way of stopping further pursuit, for a time at least."

He reached up to a crack in the masonry and thrust his finger within it. There was a hum of hidden motors, and a heavy section of wall dropped into the passageway behind them just as the shouts of their pursuers began to grow audible again.

"Another was opened on the other side which leads into a passageway that circles and ends in a blank wall about a half-mile back," explained the ex-priest. "It is a clever thing, and was devised by Mezzar Hashin the Second when he improved the original tunnel built by his father. We have only a short distance to go now."

THE tunnel ended at the foot of a flight of narrow steps. Ascending these, they emerged in a small room, one end of which was paneled with thick glass in the center of which a metal door was set.

The ex-priest opened this door, which Buell noticed was rimmed with rubber gaskets. The room beyond, much larger than the first one, was also of steel, paneled on two sides with thick glass. A cigar-shaped boat, evidently a submarine, for it was equipped with vertical and horizontal rudders, planes, and a screw propeller, stood on a pair of high skids that slanted downward toward an arched glass panel, and Buell saw a small fish swim down into the circle of light and look inquiringly at them, its gills moving slowly, its scales glistening in the artificial light.

Alcibar closed and fastened the gasketed door.

"Like his distinguished forebears, Mezzar Hashin the Fourth thought of many things," he said. "Foreseeing that Karneter might some day be discovered and perhaps captured, he planned a mode of escape, and with it a way to destroy the conquering hosts. You now behold the result of his forethought."

He climbed the iron ladder which led to the top of the submarine. Leaning forward, he worked at a catch for a moment and swung back a heavy, circular door. Then he disappeared inside the craft. A short time after there was a throbbing hum from inside the boat and the propeller blade cut the air with a roar like that of an airplane.

The ex-priest's head appeared at the top of the ladder.

"Come," he shouted, his voice barely audible above the roar of the whirling blade.

Buell helped Doris up the ladder and Rafferty followed with Delra. Descending a small stairway that led down from the round hatch, they found themselves in a snug cabin with a round window of heavy glass on each side. At the front end of the cabin, steps led up to the steersman's seat, which was under a rounded dome, also paneled with thick glass.

"Begorry, this seems like home," said Dan. "Yez gave me the straight dope, Alcie old kid."

"Do you think you can run her?"

"Just show me what thim levers are for and I'll run her clear to Halifax. I didn't spend four years on a submarine for nothing."

Taking Dan aloft, the ex-priest explained the uses of the various wheels, buttons and levers. Then he descended. He motioned to Buell.

"Everything is in readiness now," he said. "You must come up with me and close the hatch from the inside."

"Why, aren't you going with us?" asked Buell in

surprize.

"No. My place is here in Karneter, and here I remain. The upper world offers no inducements to me."

"But you will surely be killed."

"That is my lookout. Come."

When they reached the round hatchway, Alcibar stepped over to the top of the iron ladder. He pointed to two long levers that hung down from the ceiling just above his head.

"This lever," he said, "opens the glass panel at the end of the skids and shoots the submarine out into the lake as soon as the room is half filled with water. This one," indicating the other, "sets off six enormous bombs that will blast every pane of glass between the lake and the doomed city." Suddenly he pointed toward the glass panel in the side of the room. Buell looked, and saw that a crowd of armed men was rushing toward them.

"They come," cried Alcibar, "the minions of Hashin, yelping like hounds after a fox, but this time the fox will turn on them—this time the hounds will die with their victim."

He pulled back the first lever. The panel at the end of the skids moved upward and Buell saw that the room was filling rapidly.

"Fasten the hatch," shouted Alcibar.

Buell grabbed for his legs, intending to draw him within the submarine before he could touch the deadly second lever, but the ex-priest was too quick for him. Leaping aloft, he threw his full weight on it and a terrific concussion shook the room. A wall of yellow water shot past the side panels, carrying the group of human figures before it like straws.

"Close the hatch, you fool," yelled Alcibar. "You will be shot into the lake in a few seconds! You will be drowned!"

Again Buell reached unsuccessfully for the swinging figure. The water was lapping around the sides of the craft. Suddenly he felt it sliding forward. He could not save this maniac, and there were others to think of besides himself. With a quick jerk he pulled the door shut just before the waters closed over it. . . .

"LAND ho!"

This cheery call came from Dan Rafferty in the steersman's seat some ten minutes after they had plunged beneath the lake. It had taken him that long to find out just how to get to the surface.

"Come up and I'll show yez a sight for sore eyes."

Buell and the two girls mounted the steps, and cries of joy escaped their lips at sight of Chicago's rugged skyline silhouetted against a roseate sunset that was partly obscured by the pall of winter smoke. Quite near them the Municipal Pier, its foundations sheathed in ice, jutted out into the foam-flecked water.

There were tears in the eyes of Doris Lee—tears of happiness. She nestled close to Buell.

"It all seems too impossible, too like a fairy-story, to be really true," she murmured.

Dan Rafferty, his arm around the slender form of Mary Mooney, was steering with one hand.

"Sure now, it's all too true to be impossible," he said.

Midnight Madness

A blow in the night, a man thrown overboard—by these means Carl Van Doorn mistakenly thought to secure happiness for himself

TWO men sat idly smoking on the rear deck of the yacht *Doris*. Neither had spoken for fully twenty minutes, for both were busy with their thoughts.

For three years, both had been suitors for the hand of Doris Page. Clayton Raeburn had won, despite the fact that Carl Van Doorn was immensely wealthy while he depended on a salary. Van Doorn, however, had shown himself a game loser by promptly inviting the happy couple to cruise with him to the Bermudas in the yacht he had named for the girl whom both men loved. He had been a most congenial and companionable host, and Clayton's thoughts at length resolved themselves into spoken words.

"It's been awfully good of you, Carl," he said, "inviting us on this trip, I mean, and treating us as guests of honor after—after—"

"Don't mention it, old top," Van Doorn interrupted cordially. "It has been the greatest pleasure of my life."

His face, calm and smiling in the moonlight, gave no more hint of the raging storm within his bosom than did the even, pleasant tones of his voice. Van Doorn would have made a great actor.

Raeburn rose, walked to the stern rail and tossed his glowing cigar into the water. Far off to the port side he saw a dark fringe of palm trees silhouetted against the sky, and below them a curved, silvery outline: the white, sandy beach of a tropical islet.

"A veritable fairyland," he exclaimed. "It's bed-time, but I feel —"

The sentence was never finished. Something struck him a terrific blow on the head, his knees sagged, and he sank to the deck unconscious.

Van Doorn cast a quick, sly glance about the ship. All his guests had retired. Officers and men had gone below, with the exception of the helms-man, whose voice, dimly audible above the throb-bing drone of the engines and the churn of the pro-peller, was raised in a rollicking sailors' chanty as he stood at the wheel, his eyes on the moon-silvered waves ahead. Quickly tossing his blackjack away, he picked up the huddled, inert form of Raeburn and heaved it over the rail. For a moment he saw the flash of a white face disappearing beneath the foaming water — and shuddered. The ship's bell tolled the hour of midnight as he turned away from the rail with a shrug of his shoulders, calmly lighted a cigarette, and walked to his cabin on soundless, rubber-soled shoes, his actor face a study in tranquillity.

THE Page-Van Doorn wedding was a gorgeous affair. As Doris and her husband mounted the steps of the Pullman that was to convey them to the country home in which they had decided to spend their honeymoon, a cheering group of friends waved gay farewells and wished them happiness.

Van Doorn found his bride strangely reticent after they were settled in their compartment. He made several unsuccessful attempts at conversation, then lapsed into moody silence, wondering what had come over her so suddenly. She had been cheerful and vivacious up to the moment when they boarded the train. Could it be that she had guessed? But, no. That was impossible.

Doris had guessed nothing, suspected nothing. The affair on the yacht had been too well planned and too skilfully executed for that. Raeburn had disappeared during the night. That was all any one knew. Van Doorn told his story in so plausible and straightforward a manner, how he had left his friend standing near the rail at midnight and gone to his cabin alone, that every one believed him without question. It was decided that Doris' fiance had either leaped or fallen overboard when there was no one around to see. She was thinking of a shattered dream of love—a cherished vision that had faded with the disappearance of her lover.

Carl Van Doorn had been good to her during their return from the Bermudas and throughout the long, dreary year that had intervened between the finish of that trip and their wedding. His show of sympathy and his evidently sincere grief at the loss of his friend had won her regard. For months he had dropped no hint of love or marriage, waiting with patience born of a subtle understanding of the minds of women. At the psychological moment he had spoken, and she had capitulated—with reservations.

"I do not—can not—love you, Carl," she had said, sadly. "You know that all my love was Clayton's and will be to the end of time. I suppose I must marry some one, though, so if you want me you must take me as I am."

"I will teach you to love anew," he had exclaimed as he took her in his arms and rained kisses on her unresponsive lips.

All these memories returned to her as she looked out on the swiftly moving landscape, and she wondered why she had married Carl Van Doorn. Even the touch of his hand on hers sent a feeling of loathing through her entire being.

WHEN they arrived at the station Van Doorn's worries were multiplied. His chauffeur had sent word that the car in which he had intended to meet them had been damaged in a collision and was out of commission. Then there was trouble about the baggage. His wife's trunk, containing her trousseau, was missing and could not be located, either in the baggage cars or the station. After twenty minutes spent in the telegraph office he learned that the trunk had been left behind but would be forwarded on the next train.

On his return to the waiting-room he found Doris talking to a ragged derelict who wore blue glasses that announced his affliction and carried a tray of cheap pencils.

"Come," he said, a bit petulantly. "We must take a taxi. Your trunk will be along at six this evening and I have arranged to have it delivered to the house immediately." He noticed, with surprize, that there were tears in her eyes and she seemed unusually pale. "Why, what's the matter?" he asked apprehensively. "What has this tramp said to you?"

"Oh, I am so sorry for him," she murmured. "Think of the horror of a lifetime spent in darkness."

Van Doorn extracted a roll of bills from his pocket, tossed one carelessly on the tray and hurried her out the door and into the waiting taxicab. She was trembling and tearful as they drove through the streets of the village and thence along the dusty road which led to the estate of her husband.

"You are too tender-hearted, dear," he said gently. "Don't let the story of this blind man spoil the first day of our honeymoon. There are thousands of blind men in the world with stories just as sad."

"Be patient with me, Carl, and I promise you I shall be myself presently," she replied bravely, winking away the tears.

Soon they turned into a delightful driveway which curved through artistically massed flowers and shrubbery, and drew up before a well-executed reproduction of an English country house.

They spent the afternoon roaming about the spacious grounds, and Van Doorn was pleased by the fact that Doris had regained her accustomed vivacity. Her usual sparkling wit was in evidence at their tête-à-tête dinner. Afterward, in the music room, she played the piano and sang for him in her full, sweet contralto. He seized her hands as she rose, a world of passion in his eyes.

"You are wonderful, adorable, Doris," he exclaimed, pressing her hands to his lips.

"I am tired after our journey and—and everything," she murmured.

Suddenly he crushed her in his arms, smothering her with kisses.

"Please, Carl," she gasped. "Not—not now."

"But you are—"

"I know. Please go now. You may come back to

me if you wish—at midnight."

He went into his own room, puzzled and a bit sulky, closing the connecting door with unnecessary violence. With difficulty he repressed a sudden impulse to turn and enter her room, then flung himself savagely into a chair.

"Patience, fool," he muttered. "Would you spoil everything now by haste?"

A glance at his watch revealed the fact that it was not quite nine o'clock. Three hours until midnight. And why had she said "midnight"? he wondered. He lighted a cigarette and pondered the matter.

An hour passed during which he consumed one cigarette after another. That hour seemed like an age as his watch slowly ticked off the seconds. He removed his clothing and put on pajamas and slippers, then resumed his seat in the chair and tried to read. Presently he fell asleep. Wild dreams disturbed his slumber and he tossed restlessly. One dream in particular caused him to moan and cry out in his sleep—the vision of a white face going down—down beneath the blue-green water.

HE AWOKE with a start, bathed in a cold perspiration, the horror of that dream fixed in his consciousness. A chill of horror ran the length of his spine. This would not do. He must pull himself together.

For the moment he had forgotten his tryst with

his wife. His watch, lying on the dresser, showed one minute of twelve. Opening the door of her room, he looked in. She had extinguished her light and her bed was bathed in the silver rays of the moon shining in through the window.

He closed the door and stepped softly to her bedside. How pale her face looked, there in the moonlight, against the folds of wavy hair that were spread on her pillow! Somehow it reminded him of another face — a pallid face surrounded by whirling, foaming water--and he shuddered.

The mood passed quickly, however, and was followed by one of exultation. She was his — all his! The blood surged to his temples. His brain reeled with the mad intoxication of her nearness as he bent to take her in his arms. Suddenly he leaped back from the bed with a gasp of dread amazement. Instead of the soft, warm body of his wife, he had clasped to his bosom a cold corpse!

Doris dead? Impossible! What could have killed her? Had she taken her own life? At length he grew conscious of an acrid odor in the room and saw the cause. A half-emptied bottle of carbolic acid stood on the dressing-table. With a wild sob he gripped it in his shaking fingers and poured the searing liquid down his throat. He sank to the floor in agony as the great clock in the hall announced the hour of midnight.

DOWN at the railway station, a blind man boarded the midnight train. A blow on the head had gradually robbed him of his sight, and months of exposure on a tropical island had browned and dried his skin like parchment. Even his closest friends would scarcely have recognized him as Clayton Raeburn!

The Gallows Tree

Like some foul fungus grown in charnel bed,
    Sprung up between the darkness and the dawn,
A fearful tree has reared its naked head,
    But without aid of seed or spore or spawn.

One leafless limb with hempen tendril on
    Its barren tip, ensnares a visage dread.
    The tree has fruited, and the fruit is dead;
A tree that knew not seed nor spore nor spawn.

As if by some unhallowed instinct led,
    Or by some gruesome bond of interest drawn,
A host of croaking harpies comes, is fed,
    Leaves naught but whitened bones, and then is
        gone.
All barren stands the tree that bore the dead,
    A tree that left no seeds nor spores nor spawn,

The Demon of Tlaxpam

"A TABLE for wan, *señor?* I 'ave ver' ex'lent place where the *señor* can see those dance girl do —"

"No."

Standing just within the doorway of Mexican Joe's notorious café, Bart Leslie scarcely noticed the diminutive head waiter, bowing solicitously before him. Leisurely, yet with piercing intentness, his eyes swept the smoke-clouded room, hovering for a moment at each table. The contortions of a dancing girl in flaming costume, slender hands on lissom hips, mantilla flying, tiny feet keeping time with the throbbing music of a brown-skinned orchestra, drew only a cursory glance from him.

"Per 'aps the *señor* likes company. Yes? A table for two in a quiet corner, an' I send you wan ver' beautiful —"

"No! Where's Mexican Joe?"

"Ees talk weeth some friend upstair. You

weesh—?"

"Tell him Bart Leslie wants to see him, *muy pronto! Sabe?*"

"*Si, señor. Gracias, señor.*"

Deftly catching the silver dollar which Leslie had flipped to him, he sped away among the tables and hastily climbed the stairway which led to a gallery over the orchestra platform and thence to the gaming-rooms above.

Leslie rolled a cigarette, lighted it, and waited. Presently he took a tightly wadded slip of yellow paper from his vest pocket, unfolded it, and scanned the contents. It was a Western Union telegram, and the date was the day previous:

MR. BART LESLIE
BONITA
DO ME THE HONOR TO DINE WITH ME AT MEXICAN JOE'S TOMORROW EVENING AT EIGHT. I HAVE AN IMPORTANT COMMUNICATION.
                              HERNANDEZ

Leslie folded and pocketed the missive once more, then glanced at his watch. It showed five minutes past 8. Time and place were correct, but where was Hernandez? And which Hernandez? He had known two—one a vaquero formerly employed on the Bar-X Ranch, the other an ex-captain of the

Gila Men, a dread order of bandits, counterfeiters, kidnapers and murderers which he had helped to wipe out some time before.

His meditations were interrupted by the obsequious approach of the head waiter, followed by a short, wizened Mexican whose forehead was creased by a livid scar, and whom he instantly recognized as Mexican Joe.

The latter was effusive in his greeting.

"Ah, *Señor* Leslie, I am delight! I am honor, to 'ave the great Two-Gun Bart, the great Devil-Fighter, weeth us! Don Arturo ees wait for you een wan private alcove. Myself, I weel show you the way."

Considering that this same wily Mexican had once tried to drug him for a few paltry dollars, Leslie imagined that he was anything but delighted by his presence.

"All right, Joe, lead on," he said tersely. Then, loosening his two six-shooters in their holsters, both as a precaution and as a hint that he was prepared for treachery, Leslie followed the café proprietor between the tables and behind the orchestra platform to where a double row of curtained alcoves served as private dining-rooms for the more fastidious or secretive of the resort's patrons.

Pausing before one of these, he gently called:

"Don Arturo."

"*Si?*"

"*Señor* Leslie ees arrive."

" *Bueno!*"

The curtains parted and a tall, handsome Mexican, resplendent in purple velvet liberally trimmed with silver braid and adorned with buttons of the same metal, appeared in the opening and held out a slim hand, on one finger of which a dazzling ruby sparkled.

"*Buenas noches, Señor Leslie,*" he greeted.

"May God give the same to you, *Señor Capitan,*" replied Leslie, instantly recognizing Hernandez as a former officer of the dreaded Gilas.

After the handshake they entered the booth and were seated at opposite sides of the narrow table.

"No longer am I a capitan, *amigo,*" said Hernandez, taking a frost-covered cocktail-shaker from the table and rattling its contents. "Only plain Don Arturo Hernandez, a civilian in the employ of my government."

"A decided improvement, I should say," replied Leslie, "and judging from that go-to-hell outfit you're wearing, you're making it pay."

Hernandez smiled.

"Ees not so bad," he replied, removing the top from the shaker. "I 'ave concoct wan dreenk which I 'ope you weel like. Those Manhattan an' Bronchitis cocktails I don' care for, an' I know you don' drink those tequila an' mescal, so I meex a dreenk where we meet on common ground."

He filled Leslie's glass, then his own.

"To unending friendship, *amigo*," he proposed.

Leslie bowed and drank the toast.

"A corking good Bacardi cocktail, if I'm a judge," he said. "Common ground is right! If your communication is as pleasing as your cocktail, we'll get along."

"It ees from my government," replied Hernandez, producing a large sealed envelope from his pocket, "an' it may be explain' quite briefly, though the details are here."

A waiter entered with the first course of the Mexican dinner accompanied by the usual plate of steaming tortillas. When he had departed Hernandez continued :

"My government was ver' mooch impress' by the way you clean out those Gila," he said, "an' such word has come to the capital of your prowess an' exploit along the border that they 'ave send me to request your co-operation in a matter weeth which they are unable to cope."

"Before you go any farther," said Leslie, "I may as well tell you that I am still in the United States Secret Service, and all my time and efforts belong to my government."

"That ees all arrange', *amigo*, in advance. My government 'as already approach and receive permission from yours to use your service eef we can make the satisfactory arrangement weeth you. It ees for you alone to say, now."

"I see. You believe in preparedness. Well, what's the racket?"

"It ees wan ver' dangerous beezness. Near a town call' Tlaxpam many people die now, for two years — ver' sudden, ver' horrible death. They walk or ride along trail. All sudden, zeep! The head, she ees gone! Cut-off, sleeck like wan whistle! Horse come to town weeth headless body or weethout rider many time. Travelers find bloody corpse along the road weethout head. Others say they 'ave seen Satanás heemself lurking een the bushes. Wan *peón* heard a horrible laugh joost after a man was beheaded.

"Government send men to investigate. Zeep! They sometimes lose the head, too. They send the *Rurales*. Some *Rurales* also lose the head, but of thees murderer they can not find even wan track. Ees damn' bad beezness, I tal you."

"Sounds like a fairy-story to me."

"Maybe, but if you find thees fairy for my government they weel pay you twenty thousand pesos and all expenses."

"Well. That sounds substantial enough. Let me see the papers."

Hernandez broke the seal of the envelope and handed him two documents. One was permission from the American officials for Leslie to spend sixty days in Mexico whenever he should elect to go. The other was from the Mexican government, commending his past unofficial services in ridding them of the Gilas, and offering him the reward mentioned by Hernandez. All expenses were to be paid regardless of whether or not he succeeded.

The Mexican watched him narrowly as he read and folded the last document.

"Ees all satisfy, *amigo?*" he asked.

"All Jake," Leslie replied.

"You weel go?"

"Of course."

"*Caspita!* I tol' my government you're not afraid of those devil heemself. Put heem there!"

Silently the two men shook hands across the table.

2

"SON of wan gun! You tromp my ten-spot weeth a queen, eh? How you like that, an' that, an' that? Pay me."

"High, low, Jack. That's plenty." Bart Leslie fished in his pocket for a moment, then brought forth a handful of change, part of which he tossed on the table before Hernandez. Then he looked out the window of the private car furnished by the Mexican government to facilitate their journey to Tlaxpam. "Ought to be there soon, hadn't we?" he asked.

"Five minute more, maybe. Wan more hand?"

"No thanks. Have to be getting my things together."

Walking unsteadily to his sleeping-compartment, for the car lurched violently at every step, he closed and strapped his bag and handed it to the porter. Hernandez followed after gathering up the cards, and together they made their way to the platform.

"So this is Tlaxpam!"

Leslie looked out over a small group of sun-baked adobe buildings, then clutched the rail as the train halted with a jerk. He observed that the streets were deserted and remembered that it was the lazy hour of the *siesta*. Even the dogs slept.

"Eees the end of wan journey — the beginning of another. Follow me, *amigo*."

Hernandez stepped down from the platform and led the way around the corner of the station, the porter following with their bags. Here a driver slept peacefully behind the wheel of an ancient and badly battered touring-car.

Hernandez shook him awake.

"*Alerta, hombre!*" he roared. "*Mil demonios!* Did I hire you to sleep for me?"

The man awoke, then took their bags from the grinning porter.

"Pardon, Don Arturo. I did not hear the train arrive."

"You sleep like an ox. Be off, then. You have your orders."

After considerable persuasion with crank and primer, the engine started noisily, and they rattled off down a narrow, dusty street. Presently they stopped before one of the larger adobe houses, the door of which was opened by a dark-skinned *mozo* as soon as they had stepped down from the tonneau.

After a bath, and a meal served by the same dusky servant, Leslie and Hernandez entered the patio to enjoy their cigars, and found comparative coolness on a bench beneath the spreading branches of a huge pecan tree.

"And now, *señor*," inquired Hernandez, politely, "how soon will you be willing to start on thees dangerous beezness?"

"Start? I have already started. What I want to do is to continue, and the sooner the better."

The Mexican puffed reflectively for a moment.

"You Americans are so eempetuous. Maybe you 'ave not notice something, eh? I breeng you here during the hour of the *siesta*. I speak not your name, but call you only *'amigo'* een front of my *mozos*. For why? Thees fairy, as you call heem, may 'ave the spy any place. Een my very house! Eef he know you are here you are mark for death before you start. *Sabe?*"

"I see. You want me at least to get one chance at

him before he bumps me off. But what makes you think he has spies?"

"Those other come. Zeep! They lose the head too damn' queek. I don' like. They come weeth beeg noise and brag *muy mucho.* You come weethout noise and maybe do something. When they come everybody know. When you come, only I know. Ees not bad idea, eh?"

"Excellent logic, I should say. In any event it would be taking needless chances to herald my coming and my errand. But how and when do I start after your friend? 'Ogre' would perhaps be a better name."

"Tonight at midnight. Between now and that time you weel get all the rest and sleep you can. At 12 I weel 'ave a guide and horses to take you into the danger zone. Twelve picked men, armed to the teeth and carrying provisions and equipment, weel follow a half-mile behind you. They weel rush to your aid at the sound of a shot, and weel be subject to your command at all times. I 'ave arrange weeth a friend to quarter you een case you find it necessary to make camp. And now, *amigo,* weel you 'ave a leetle *siesta* before dinner?"

Bart Leslie tossed his cigar butt into the shrubbery, stretched his powerful arms, and grinned.

"That's the best thing you've said today," he replied.

3

FROM some near-by tower a bell tolled the hour of 11. Leslie, who had retired immediately after dinner, was aroused from a sound slumber. He pushed back the covers and sat up in bed, trying to think what it was that had awakened him. Then the sound was repeated—a gentle tapping at his door.

Whipping one of his guns from the holster that swung from the belt on the chair beside him, he rose and tip-toed to the door.

"*Que gente?*" he asked. "Who is it?"

"Open, *amigo*," came back the soft reply. "Ees Hernandez."

"Ahead of your schedule, aren't you?" asked Leslie as he swung the door back.

To his surprize, there was no one in sight. About to step out into the dark hallway, he suddenly changed his mind as the sound of subdued breathing came to him from the right. Instinctively he knew there was someone crouching beside the door.

The warning of Hernandez flashed through his mind. Death, he was positive, lurked there in the corner of the hall—the mysterious and horrible end that had overtaken his predecessors.

He must act, that was sure. But how? To shoot through the wall would be to arouse the household—perhaps the community—and if the wall were brick-lined the bullet might be ineffective. A heavy mahogany chair standing beside the door gave him an idea. He knew that a scant two feet separated the edge of the doorway and the corner of the hall, hence he could calculate, with reasonable precision, the position of his concealed enemy.

First tucking his gun beneath his pajama belt, he quietly picked up the heavy chair by the back. Then, turning it so the front of the seat was forward, he swung it aloft and brought it down with crushing force at the point where he calculated the man's head would be.

As the chair struck a solid object a grunt of surprize and pain came from the corner, a heavy body pitched downward across the doorway, and a large machete clattered to the tile floor.

Before Leslie could find the switch to turn on his own light another flashed on in the hallway. There followed the patter of feet and a muttered exclamation in Spanish.

"*Madre de Dios!* They have keel the American already!"

"You mistake, Carlos. It is only a *peón.*"

Leslie lowered his gun as he saw Hernandez and another Mexican, both in their sleeping-garments and carrying revolvers, rushing toward him.

"What ees happen, *amigo?*" the former asked him.

Leslie leaned nonchalantly on the back of the

chair and mechanically reached toward his breast pocket for his makings, then remembered he was still attired in his pajamas, and grinned.

"That *hombre* knocked on my door and I thought it was you, so I opened it. When I found he was hiding in the corner I figured he wasn't friendly, so I quieted him with this chair."

"Ees plenty quiet, I tal you," said Hernandez, bending over the prostrate man, who was barefooted and wore the simple white cotton jacket and pantaloons of the same material common to Mexicans of the poorest class. "I theenk maybe you 'ave keel heem. Let us see." He turned him over on his back and a livid bruise on his forehead showed where the heavy chair had struck. Hernandez fingered this for a moment, then placed his ear to the fellow's heart. "Ees alive," he announced, "an' stunned." Turning to his companion, he said in Spanish. "Bind and gag him, Carlos. Perhaps we can make him talk when he revives."

The man called Carlos threw the would-be assassin over his shoulder as if he had been a sack of grain, and carried him off down the hallway.

"May as well dress now," said Leslie. "We can't get much sleep before midnight."

Hernandez shrugged.

"Joost as well," he replied. "Meet me downstairs when you are ready."

Some time later Leslie, wearing full cowboy attire and two businesslike forty-fives, stepped into the spacious living-room. Finding it untenanted, he sat down on a divan and rolled a cigarette. A full twenty minutes elapsed before Hernandez entered.

"Ees no use," he said. "That damn' *peón* don't talk."

"Came to, did he?"

"*Si*, some time ago. We threaten weeth the hot iron—everytheeng. No use. Says he don't know about these head-stealers."

"What's his story?"

"Says he came only to rob the rich *Americano*."

"But he carried a machete."

"To be sure. Eef you 'ad step through that door-- zeep! We find you weethout the head. Those damn' fairy are wise already, I bat you. Per'aps you better not leave tonight, *amigo*."

"Fast little workers, aren't they? Crave action. Well, let's give 'em some. Keep that *hombre* here and get him to talk if you can, but meanwhile let me take the trail. I'm not going to be scared off by a sneaking *peón* with a machete."

"But, *señor*, it ees more dangerous than ever, now. A little later we might—"

"Nix on the *mañana* stuff. I'm going right now if you can get someone to guide me. Are your men afraid to go?"

Hernandez shrugged.

"My men are brave," he replied, "but it ees

sometimes best to meex brains weeth bravery. Go then, eef you are determine', but remember, *amigo*. I warned you." He clapped his hands and the man Carlos appeared in the doorway. "Send José," he ordered, "and saddle the horses. José Gonzaga," he explained to Leslie, "weel guide you. Ees three-quarter Indian, and speaks no English, so you weel 'ave to converse in the Spanish."

A moment later a tall, swarthy fellow entered. Although he wore the dress of a Mexican vaquero, his high cheekbones, hawk nose and dark skin be-spoke a predominance of Aztec blood. He was beardless, and three livid scars, two on the right cheek and one on the forehead, added to the feroc-ity of his countenance. For armament he carried a knife and revolver, both stuck in his sash, a carbine slung across his back, and two well-filled cartridge belts.

"*Buenas noches, señores*," he greeted with a flash of dazzling white teeth.

When both had made the customary polite reply. Hernandez said :

"*Señor* Leslie is determined to depart tonight, de-spite the fact that our plans have been discovered. Yon will therefore start at once and I will send the men after you as agreed." He turned to Leslie and extended his hand. "*Adios, amigo*. May good fortune attend you."

Leslie shook the proffered hand.

"*Gracias, señor*," he replied. "I hope to play my cards better than I did on the train. *Adios*."

4

JOSÉ led the way through the patio to the stables in the rear. Here Carlos held two rangy Mexican ponies, saddled and ready. To Leslie he handed a carbine like that carried by the guide, and a long sheath-knife.

Swinging the gun across his back and attaching the knife to his belt, Leslie mounted and rode forth, followed by José. The latter took the lead as they threaded the narrow streets, lighted only by the waning moon. Later, when they emerged into the open country, they rode side by side.

At first they crossed a waste of sand, gleaming a dull silver in the moonlight and dotted here and there with desert growths—giant cacti that reared their armlike branches heavenward as if in a constant appeal for water, scrawny twisted mesquite in scattered clumps, and the more lowly prickly pears, their barbed and segmented branches twined and interlaced like the tentacles of cuttle-fish.

Later their trail led through a group of rocky hills, and thence along the bank of a narrow, tree-bordered stream, enclosed by towering canyon walls. When they entered the canyon, José paused.

"It is here, *señor*," he announced, "that the land

of the demons begins. On this spot, just three nights ago, a headless body was found."

"And no trace of the murderer was discovered?"

"None. A riderless horse, blood-splattered and weary, wandered into Tlaxpam the next morning, and we knew what we would find, even before I started here with two companions. There was but one fresh trail — that of the horse that had borne the victim."

"Is the trail so little used?"

"Yes, *señor*, since the mysterious murders commenced. Formerly it was quite popular with those entering and leaving Tlaxpam from the north. Now it is shunned as a plague spot, although a detour of five miles is necessary to avoid this pass. Only strangers, travelers unacquainted with its bloody history, use it now, and these seldom live to boast of it. Many of these have been warned, have laughed at the warning, and have paid for their foolhardiness with their heads. A few who have escaped swear that they heard the whistling of the wings of Satan, who swooped down at them without warning, and whose frightful attack they avoided only by the utmost quickness and haste in riding away. Others claim to have heard his horrible, blood-curdling laugh, and still others to have seen him lurking in the undergrowth."

"There are many people with powerful imaginations," replied Leslie. "How long is this pass?"

"Nearly a mile. From now on we are in grave danger. Shall we proceed at once, or wait until daylight?"

"Let us go on."

Scarcely had these words passed the lips of the American than both men heard a noise in the pass ahead of them. Mingled with the distant clatter of horses' hoofs they heard someone singing or yelling—perhaps both—and the sounds were punctuated with the reports of a gun.

"Some drunken fool," said José. "Ah! The sounds have stopped. Perhaps the demons have killed him."

The sounds of voice and gun had died, but the patter of hoofs was still audible. There sounded, however, another voice, high-pitched, cackling, as if in demoniac laughter.

"*Santo Dios!* The laugh of Satanás!" cried José.

"Pull over to that side of the road, quick!" ordered Leslie. "I'll wait on this side."

They had not long to wait. The hoofbeats slowed down from a gallop to a singlefoot. A horse appeared, rounding a bend in the canyon wall, but the animal was without a rider.

"*Demonios!* It has happened!" exclaimed José, crossing himself devoutly. "*Maria Madre* preserve us!"

Leslie caught the bridle of the riderless horse and, producing his flashlight, examined the saddle

Otis Adelbert Kline

and the back of the beast. Both were spattered with blood.

"The body will be lying near the point where the singing ceased," said José. " Of that I am certain."

Again came the thunder of hoofbeats, this time from behind them.

"Our men are coming," José said. "They heard the shots and think we need help."

"Here, take the reins and bring the men forward when they arrive," ordered Leslie. "I'm going to look for the body and the murderer."

He spurred his pony forward. A short distance beyond the first bend he saw a ghastly thing in the moonlight—a headless body lying by the roadside. Dismounting, he brought his flashlight into play. There were no tracks of human being or animal near the body, other than those made by himself, his horse, and the horse of the victim. He walked ahead for fifty feet, then discovered a revolver in the dust of the road. Five of the six chambers had been discharged. Pocketing this, he again made his way forward. A walk of a quarter of a mile revealed no tracks other than those made by the victim's horse, and he knew the tragedy had not occurred that far back. Puzzled, he mounted and rode back to where José and the twelve men sent by Hernandez waited beside the body. The guide had dismounted and was standing beside the corpse.

"You found tracks of the murderer, *señor?*" he

asked.

"Not a track."

"That was to be expected. I have found a paper on the body of this young fool, explaining why he rode through the pass. It seems he made a drunken wager with another young blood that he could come through unscathed. The paper is the other man's guarantee of the payment of a hundred pesos by this fellow's bank in case his headless body is found. What is to be done?"

"From what town did this man ride?"

"Rosario."

"Tie the body on the horse and let two of our men take it back to his relatives. Put the paper in the pocket where you found it."

When the two riders and the horse with its ghastly burden had been dispatched in accordance with his orders, Leslie posted his men by twos at intervals of a thousand feet along the canyon. Then, accompanied by Jose, he patrolled the road for the remainder of the night.

The first faint streaks of dawn found Leslie and his companion near the center of the danger zone. The former reined his horse to a halt as the odor of burning wood came to his nostrils.

"Someone is making camp near here," he said. "I smell smoke."

José smiled.

"It is only Tio Luis, the Anciano," he replied,

"preparing his breakfast."

"Uncle Louis, the Old One? Who is he?"

"The Anciano is a very venerable hermit who braves the dangers of this pass to remain with the holy shrine of San Antonio, which he has attended since the death of good Father Salvador some years ago. Although he is but a lay brother, he is a most holy man, revered by all who know him, and a very good friend of *Señor* Hernandez. He has agreed to quarter our men if we find it necessary to remain."

"A shrine of St. Anthony here? But why has it not been moved?"

"Because it rests on a holy spot, venerated for more than two centuries. From a crevice in the hillside, just beside the niche containing the image of the saint, there flows a spring. This spring empties into a shallow pool where the sick have come to bathe for many generations and where countless miracles of healing have occurred. Whereas pilgrims often came alone in former years and at all hours, they now come only in the middle of the day and in considerable numbers for mutual protection on account of the murderous fiends who surround this place. Did not *Señor* Hernandez mention the Anciano?"

"He only said quarters had been provided for the men. How do we reach this place?"

"We have only to ride up the ravine at your left, down which this small stream trickles. It is the overflow from the sacred pool."

5

LESLIE assembled his men and led them up the steep path in the winding ravine which had been pointed out by José. Presently he emerged on a small plot of more even ground and beheld the home of the Anciano. It was a small abode hut, built against the steep hillside. On the left of the hut was a niche containing a life-size image of St. Anthony, and just in front of the image was the pool described by his guide, which was fed by a spring that bubbled from the rock. From a battered and rusty stovepipe that protruded from the side of the hut, there issued the wood smoke which was being wafted down the ravine, and which had drawn Leslie's attention to the place.

At the right of the enclosure was a long, low shed, open on one side and built from wide, rough, unpainted boards. This was evidently intended to quarter the horses of pilgrims as well as the pilgrims themselves, for rings were fastened at frequent intervals along the back wall.

The men tethered their horses and busied themselves with opening packs, preparing breakfast, and pitching tents, while Leslie and José went up to the hut of the anchorite. It was evident that he had heard their arrival, for a bent figure, attired in a ragged robe of rusty brown and leaning on a staff, emerged from the doorway and hobbled forward to meet them. As he drew near, Leslie saw a face that was seamed, wrinkled and emaciated above an unkempt gray beard.

The hermit paused before them and leaned on his staff.

"God bless you, my sons," he mumbled, with the peculiar sibilant enunciation that invariably denotes the paucity or absence of teeth. "You have come from my friend, *Señor* Hernandez, I presume. And you have passed the demons unscathed. *Deo gracias.*"

"Unscathed thus far, Tio Luis," replied José. "This is *Señor* Leslie, the great Devil-Fighter, who has come to rid us of the demons that haunt this vicinity."

"*Bueno!* We have need of him, and our prayers for his safety and success will go with him on his dangerous mission. But come within and join me at breakfast if you can do with my humble fare."

They accompanied the aged hermit to the door of the hut, where he politely stood aside and bade them enter.

"All that you see is yours, my sons," he said as he followed them into the small front room. "Excuse me while I go into the kitchen to see about breakfast."

He hobbled through a curtained doorway into the rear room, and Leslie heard him puttering about to the accompanying clatter of pans and crockery.

José unslung his carbine, stood it in a corner, and flung himself into one of the chairs beside the bare table that stood in the center of the room.

"*Huy*, but I am tired," he grunted. "It has been a strenuous night, señor.

Leslie politely agreed with him, disposed of his own carbine, and took a chair on the other side of the table. While he waited for the puttering anchorite he glanced around the room. The furnishings were meager enough to suit the taste of the most humble of lay brothers; a low cot covered by a frowsy blanket, four crude chairs, and the table at which they sat, its bare top stained with food and beverages. Beneath the single window there stood a small, crudely constructed pulpit on which lay a book, evidently a missal. Both pulpit and book were covered with much dust, evidence that they had known little if any use since the passing of Father Salvador. The plastered walls were cracked, grimy, and festooned with cobwebs.

Presently the Anciano limped through the curtained doorway. Again apologizing for the meanness of the fare, he set before them some boiled rice, a huge chunk of honeycomb, and hot chocolate.

After consulting with José and the anchorite, Leslie decided to post two guards at each end of the pass for the morning, do a little exploring on his own account, and permit the other men to rest, relieving the guards at noon.

Accordingly, he set out after breakfast, resolved to make a minute examination of the scene of the tragedy enacted the night before, hoping that the morning sunlight might reveal some clue overlooked in his search by flashlight.

Arriving at the place where the foolhardy rider had been beheaded, he dismounted and scanned every foot of the ground in the vicinity. The road, at that point, was less than ten feet in width. On one side the cliff rose almost perpendicularly to a height of nearly twenty-five feet, and appeared unscalable. On the other, the stony ground sloped sharply to the water's edge. Some thirty feet from the point where the blood spots began, a clump of stunted willows had found foothold in the rocky bank. Leslie peered into these with a view to ascertaining whether or not they had been used for purposes of ambush, then uttered a cry of surprize at sight of a bloodstained object hanging among them. He drew it forth and recognized it instantly as the outer edge of a broad-brimmed sombrero. It appeared to have been cut from the hat by a very keen instrument, not in the form of a circle or oval, but more like an irregular hexagon, no two lines being equal but all lines straight, or nearly so. He noticed, also, that it was creased at each point where two straight cuts joined. An examination of the bushes revealed the fact that they had not been used as a hiding-place by a human being.

Puzzled, Leslie hung the blood-caked relic over his saddle-horn, mounted, and rode back to camp.

His men, with the exception of one who had been left on guard by José, were sleeping beneath the tents, the walls of which had been raised to admit the breeze. The guard took charge of his horse and looked curiously at the bloody hat-brim which Leslie removed from the saddle-horn.

He started for the hut of the hermit, intending to show his find to that individual, then paused as the sudden clatter of hoofbeats came from behind him.

Turning, he beheld one of his men emerging from the ravine. The fellow dismounted and ran to where he was standing, fear and horror written on his bronzed features. So great was his agitation that, although his lips worked spasmodically, he was unable to speak.

"Well, what is it?" snapped Leslie. "Have you lost your voice?"

The man crossed himself and muttered beneath his breath.

"*Maria Madre* preserve us!" he gasped. "We are all doomed men."

"But how? Speak to the point."

"The demons! They kill in broad daylight now!"

"Where? Who?"

"We were standing guard at the north end of the pass, Miguel and I. They have beheaded Miguel!"

Otis Adelbert Kline

"What did *they* look like?"

"I did not see them, *señor*."

"What? Your comrade slain before your eyes and you could not see the murderers?"

"Not before my eyes, *señor*. I — that is — "

"You were sleeping, I suppose, on duty."

The fellow hung his head.

"We were very tired, Miguel and I, after the night's vigil. Things were so peaceful that we decided there could be no harm in our snatching a little sleep, one at a time. I stood guard for two hours while Miguel slept. Then he mounted guard, but it seemed I had scarcely closed my eyes before I heard him utter a choking cry. I caught up my carbine and leaped instantly to my feet. Before my eyes the headless body of my comrade slipped from his saddle, and at the same moment I heard the whir of wings above my head! Although I looked upward instantly, I saw nothing!"

"This whir of wings. Was it loud like the roar of an airplane?"

"No, *señor*. It had a much quieter tone, like the whistle of a large bird's pinions. "

"What has happened, my sons?"

Wheeling, Leslie saw the Anciano. who had hobbled up unnoticed, behind him.

6

LESLIE explained the situation to the hermit and showed him the hatbrim he had found.

"Lend us the wisdom of your years, Tio Luis," he requested. "This is the most singular as well as the most hellish thing I have ever encountered. What do you make of it?"

The old man turned the gruesome relic in his bony hands, squinting at it with watery eyes.

"A man beheaded, the whir of wings—and this." He shook his head, handed the thing back to Leslie, and crossed himself. "I fear you are playing with fire that will destroy you, my sons. We have a saying: 'He must have iron fingers who would flay the devil.' "

"We also have a saying that is apt, Tio Luis," Leslie replied. " 'Give the devil rope enough and he'll hang himself.' " He turned to the guard. "Saddle my horse, Pedro, and arouse José. We'll see if the devil has left any more souvenirs."

Once more the anchorite shook his grizzled head.

" 'He was slain who had warning, not he who took it,' " he quoted. "You have my sympathy, my son—that and my prayers."

"The former is premature, but for the latter I thank you," replied Leslie. "Ready, Pedro?"

"*Sí, señor.* José will be out in a moment. He is pulling on his boots."

José emerged from the tent as Leslie started toward the horses. Together, they mounted and rode down the ravine.

They covered the half-mile to the north end of the canyon at a brisk gallop. The body of the slain man lay sprawled in the middle of the road, and his patient horse stood near by, apparently not greatly frightened by the diabolical presence which had given Pedro so much alarm.

Dismounting, both men looked carefully for tracks of the slayer, but their search was as fruitless as before. Nor was there a cut hat-brim, such as Leslie had found on the scene of the last tragedy.

Compelled at last to give up their hopeless search, they tied the body of Miguel across his saddle and took it back to camp. Leslie directed that the corpse be rolled in an extra tent-fly and sent to Tlaxpam with one of the men. Then he detailed two guards for the north end of the pass and two to relieve those at the south end, warning them to take heed from the death of Miguel and do no sleeping on duty. These matters attended to, he instructed the camp guard to call him before sundown, and retired to his tent for a much-needed rest.

It seemed to Leslie that he had not slept more than fifteen minutes when he was aroused by a tug at his blanket. Opening his eyes, he saw José standing over him.

"The sun nears the horizon, *señor*," he said, "and the Anciano has bidden us to sup with him. Some pilgrims visited the shrine this afternoon and left gifts for the holy man. Among them were a pullet and a bottle of wine he desires to share with us."

"Pilgrims? Who were they?"

"Only two *peóns* with their wives. They came here on donkeys from a hacienda near Tlaxpam, and departed after they had bathed in the sacred pool and deposited their gifts."

"I see. Tell the Anciano we accept with gratitude. A pullet and a bottle of wine will be preferable to *tasajo* and *frijoles*. I'll be along in a few minutes."

José departed, and Leslie pulled on his boots. Then he buckled his two gun-belts about him and stepped out of the tent, intending to wash for dinner at the spring. His men were squatting or lying around their cooking-fires, preparing their evening meal.

As he rounded the last of the tents he saw a man disrobing beside the sacred pool. On closer approach he recognized Pedro.

"What's the matter? Sick?" he inquired.

"A bath in the pool at sunset is said to cure boils," replied the Mexican, stripping off his shirt. "I have two on my back, *señor*."

"At sunset? I didn't know the time made any difference."

"Oh, but it does, *señor*. The Anciano told me so himself."

Walking past the image of St. Anthony, Leslie

laved his face and hands in the bubbling spring. Then, much refreshed, he started for the hermit's hut. The sun was sinking, and he heard the splashing of Pedro as the lad entered the pool.

Rounding the corner of the hut, Leslie came upon José seated on the doorstep smoking a husk cigarette. In the kitchen he heard the anchorite bustling about among his pots and pans. The table was set and graced by a wide, wicker-covered bottle with a long neck.

"How is your appetite, José?" he asked.

"Like that of a wolf, *señor*. And yours?"

"Like that of a pack of wolves. I'm accustomed to eating lunch, but I've been too busy today."

At the sound of their voices the hermit limped out from the kitchen.

"Come in, my sons," he said. "Be seated and sample this wine with me while the pullet reaches the right degree of tenderness."

They obeyed his invitation with alacrity.

"This is really an imposition, Tio Luis," said Leslie as the old man filled their glasses, "but I couldn't resist. I promise you a dozen pullets and a dozen bottles to replace these when I get back to Tlaxpam."

"I, also, "cried José, eagerly reaching for his glass. "We are eternally indebted to you. I propose the health of our host, *señor*."

The hermit bowed, smiled, sipped his wine, and

rose. "I must look to our food," he said.

The two men sipped their wine and discussed the events of the day. Presently José emptied his glass and refilled it.

Then the anchorite entered again. In one hand he bore a large pot from which savory odors exuded. In the other he carried a deep plate over which a bowl had been inverted. Placing pot and plate on the table, he lifted the bowl.

"Chicken and chile!" cried José. "Food for a king."

"And *tortillas!*" exclaimed Leslie. "Did you bake them yourself?"

His words were followed by a shout from outside — then an excited babel of voices.

Leslie put down his glass and rushed out the door. He saw a man standing beside the sacred pool. The others, aroused from their places beside the campfires, were running toward their companion. He joined the rush to the pool and saw, in a moment, the cause of the commotion. A half-clothed, headless body with arms outstretched lay on the very rim of the pool.

"It is Pedro!" a man cried. "The demons have slain Pedro!"

"They will slay us all if we remain," said another. "I'm going back to Tlaxpam."

"And I."

"And I."

José came running.

"What has happened, *señor?*" he asked, his tongue a bit thickened by wine.

"We've lost another man." Leslie produced his flashlight and snapped it on. "See if you can quiet these sniveling cowards while I have a look around."

7

WHILE José, rendered eloquent and perhaps more fearless by the wine he had consumed, sought to quiet the fears of his comrades, Leslie made a thorough examination of the body. He judged from its position that Pedro had been seated on the rim of the pool with his back to the image, dressing, when the crime occurred. The other men, occupied with their evening meal, would not have seen the attack because of the tents intervening between the cooking-fires and the pool.

Using the jutting rocks for feet and hands, he next climbed the steep hillside at the left of the image, circled the point over the niche, and descended on the right side, searching every inch of the way with his flashlight. As there were no tracks other than those he had made himself, he concluded that the attack had not come from above. It was useless to look for tracks on the hard-packed ground around the pool, and there seemed to be no other clues.

His men, he noticed, were gathered in a small group around the loquacious José, and he was about to snap off his flashlight and go to the guide's assistance when the white circle fell on something that gave him pause. It was a large drop of blood on the stone floor of the niche, and directly in front of the image. With a low cry of surprize he bent over to examine it, then leaped up and whirled about, gun in hand, at the sound of a footfall behind him. He returned the weapon to its holster with a nervous laugh as he saw the Anciano standing there, peering at him with his little watery eyes.

"Sorry, Tio Luis," he apologized, "but you gave me a deuce of a start."

"Do not mention it, my son," replied the hermit. "I should have announced my coming at a time like this. So the demons have profaned the sacred pool! Now, indeed, will the wrath of God smite them. You have found a clue?"

"Only a drop of the blood on the floor of the niche. It has some significance, of course—but what? How do you suppose this blood was dropped clear over here, a full ten feet from the body? And there are no blood-spots between, other than those around the body itself."

"It is as mysterious as all else that has happened. We have a saying: 'The devil lurks behind the cross,' and if this be true he would not hesitate to conceal himself in a shrine of St. Anthony."

"That explanation may suffice for you, but it does not satisfy me," replied Leslie. Then, noticing that some of his men were saddling their horses, he hurried to the assistance of José, whose alcoholic eloquence had apparently not been sufficient to deter them from their avowed purpose of returning to Tlaxpam.

"Get down, *hombre!*" he roared, addressing a man who had already mounted. The fellow hesitated, then did as he was bidden. He swung on the others. "What does this mean? Are you women in the uniforms of fighters?"

"We can not fight the devil," one man replied.

"We shall only lose our lives and accomplish nothing by remaining," said another. "Come with us, *señor.*"

Leslie laughed.

"Go, then, cowards," he retorted. "Go back to Don Arturo and tell him you are afraid — that you are too white-livered to remain and avenge the death of your comrades. I'll stay and fight these murderers alone."

"Not alone, *señor,*" said José. "I remain with you." He appealed again to the men. "The great Devil-Fighter stays," he said, "to deal death to those who have slain our comrades. Boon companions we have been for many years, we and those of us who have died for our cause. The Devil-Fighter, whom we have only known since yesterday—who has only known Pedro and Miguel a few hours—remains to avenge them. Is there one among us who can do less?"

"He is right," said the man who had just dismounted. "I remain."

"My duty is plain," said another. "I remain also."

"And I."

"And I."

"*Viva* Leslie! Hurrah for the great Devil-Fighter!"

Thus the mutiny was quelled and order restored.

In a trice, José had set them at various tasks, knowing full well that if their hands were occupied they would have less time for fearful speculations. The body of Pedro was wrapped and swung from the rafters of the shed. The watch-fires were replenished so that most of the camp was illuminated, and men were sent to relieve the guards at the ends of the canyon.

In order to hearten his men further, Leslie decided to ride down with the two who were to take the post nearest Tlaxpam. Nothing untoward occurring after an hour's vigil with these two, he enjoined them to be on their guard and rode away to see how the two at the other end of the canyon were getting along.

He had passed the camp and was rounding the next curve at a slow canter, wrapped in meditation as he pondered the terrible and amazing events of the last twenty-four hours, when with startling suddenness there came a sound resembling the whistle of huge pinions, directly above his head.

There was no time to think—yet he acted, by instinct rather than by reason. With catlike quickness he hurled himself sideways and hung, Indian fashion, supported by one stirrup and the neck of the pony. Something struck heavily on the saddle and he heard a sharp metallic click. Then the frightened animal bounded forward so suddenly that he nearly lost his hold. Deft horseman that Leslie was, he managed to regain his seat before much ground had been covered, but nearly lost his balance in doing so, because when he reached for the saddle-horn he grasped only empty air.

Pulling the pony to a halt he dismounted, unslung his carbine, and waited for a new attack. Five minutes elapsed—ten—fifteen, yet he saw nothing save the rugged canyon bathed in the moonlight, and heard only the chirruping serenade of insects and the occasional call of a night bird.

Holding the carbine in his left hand, he felt the front of the saddle with his right. The horn, he discovered, had been sheared away smoothly and completely. Thus, he was certain, would his head have been sheared from his shoulders had he kept his seat a fraction of a second longer when that awful, death-dealing thing had hurtled down at him from a clear sky.

And the thing itself. What was it? Something conceived by man, he felt sure—for Leslie was not superstitious--yet designed with such diabolical cleverness as to kill with almost superhuman accuracy and leave no clue that would hint at its nature or *modus operandi*.

Convinced, at length, that he could not further his cause by remaining longer, Leslie removed his broad Stetson and fastened it to the saddle-ring with the chin-strap. Then he mounted with a better view of the air above his head and rode, carbine in hand, to where the two guards were posted. Finding that they had nothing to report, he left them with a warning to maintain the utmost vigilance, and rode slowly back toward the camp. While he rode, albeit he kept a weather eye for danger, he was thinking, and to such purpose that when he reached camp a new plan had completely formed in his mind. He greeted José with a disconcerting smile as that worthy came out to meet him.

8

"THE *señor* is amused?" José answered the smile of Leslie with a flash of his white teeth. "Perhaps he has discovered something."

"Nothing new, José," Leslie replied. "Just thought of a new scheme to work on this so-called 'devil'."

"And the scheme?"

"I'll show you in a minute. Go and ask Tio Luis if we may tear three or four boards off his horse-shed."

"Tio Luis retired for the night shortly after you left. Should we disturb him for such a trifle?"

"No, let him sleep, but bring four boards into my tent, a riata, and a couple of good sharp machetes. Don't make any more noise than necessary, and say nothing about this to the others."

"*Si, señor.*"

As soon as José departed to do his bidding, Leslie went behind the tents and pulled a huge armful of grass. With this he entered the rear of his own tent, deposited it on the floor, and lighted his lantern. Then he opened one of his saddle-bags and took therefrom a complete suit of cowboy attire.

José returned in a trice with the boards and the machetes.

"Now bring me a saddle," Leslie ordered.

When José got back with the saddle he found the American industriously hewing one of the broad boards with a machete. The wood was partly softened by dry rot, though firm enough not to crumble, and was consequently easily shaped with the keen blade.

Leslie finished this board, which was about six feet in length, and handed it to José.

"Cut me another the same shape," he said.

José worked swiftly, but stole a curious glance at Leslie from time to time as the latter cut one of the remaining boards into four pieces, the other into two, and then proceeded to cut holes and notches in them.

The boards shaped, Leslie cut the riata, a piece at a time, and began lashing the boards together, using the notches and holes for the purpose. When José saw a figure resembling the frame of a scarecrow beginning to take shape he grinned broadly.

"Por Dios!" he cried. "Do you expect to fool the devil with so simple a thing?"

"Wait until it's finished," Leslie answered, drawing the trousers and boots over the frame and stuffing them with grass. "Bring a horse around behind my tent while I finish this work of art."

His own effigy completed to his satisfaction, Leslie clapped his Stetson over the head and lashed the thing to the saddle with what was left of the riata. Then he lifted the rear tentflap and passed it through to the waiting José. Together they placed the dummy on the back of the surprized and annoyed pony, and stood back to view their handiwork.

"Viva!" exclaimed José. "Your double sits the horse, *señor*."

"Now for the rest of my plan," said Leslie. "I want you to saddle another horse and lead this one, giving it about twenty feet of rope. Ride very slowly up and down the canyon until the attack occurs. If we may judge by our previous experience it is almost sure to come. The enemy will attack the rear man for two reasons. One is that an attack on the man in front could be seen and perhaps frustrated by the man in the rear, and the other is that the thing looks like me in the moonlight and I have reason to believe my head would be preferred as a souvenir above all others in this company.

"While you are walking your horses on the trail below I'll follow at a distance of about a hundred yards on the cliff above. I have a pair of moccasins here that will eliminate any clatter I might make with boots and spurs, and will thus have a chance to view the attack from above while you look on from below."

"*Cáspita!* Now we will get this devil, for sure."

"I hope so. Go and saddle up while I put on my moccasins. If we have any traitors in camp they will see us ride away together. If not, there will be no harm in temporarily deceiving them. I'll throw the end of the lead rope to you from behind the tent when you're ready to start. Then I can hike over to the top of the cliff and wait for you."

As José, some moments later, rode down the arroyo apparently followed by the American, Leslie stood and viewed his handiwork with pardonable pride for a moment, then scurried up to the top of the cliff and waited for the guide to appear below him.

It was not long before what looked for all the world like two horsemen riding in single file emerged from the arroyo and started toward Tlaxpam at a leisurely pace. Following his preconceived plan, Leslie kept about three hundred feet behind them on the cliff top, his moccasined feet making no sound, his carbine held ready for action.

A full quarter of a mile had been covered when Leslie's quick eye caught the movement of a shadowy form near a clump of brush at his right. It disappeared in the bushes almost instantly, and he paused, breathlessly awaiting its reappearance. The view had been so indistinct that he was not sure whether it had been a man or an animal.

After several minutes of waiting, he grew impatient and had just decided to explore the bushes where the apparition had dropped out of sight, when he saw it again, this time fully three hundred yards away and just on the brink of the cliff. It was undeniably a man, though grotesquely shaped, a man with what looked like a huge hump on his back. As he looked, he realized that the prowler was directly above the point where José and his own effigy would be, the guide having made considerable progress while he had been waiting for the reappearance of the figure.

Dismayed at this unforeseen circumstance that

had caused him to lag so far behind the guide, Leslie rushed forward. As he did so, he was amazed to see the hump suddenly detach itself from the back of the man—no longer a hump, but something about the size of a peck measure. It was raised aloft, then hurled downward over the side of the cliff. Leslie halted and brought his carbine to his shoulder, but at this moment his quarry suddenly dropped from sight.

Cursing his own slowness, he again hurried forward, stepped into an unseen crevice, and fell sprawling, cutting his hands painfully on the sharp stones. As if in mirth at his discomfiture there came to him the raucous echoes of hideous, demoniac laughter.

He scrambled to his feet, caught a glimpse of the humpbacked figure again, and fired. Simultaneously with the crack of his rifle the figure dropped out of sight. Again he ran forward, his rifle held in readiness, straining his eyes in all directions for another sight of his quarry. He had almost come upon the spot where he judged the marauder had stood, when he caught the movement of something in the shrubbery, this time a full hundred feet back from the cliff. Again he fired and rushed forward, convinced that his bullet had found its mark. It seemed, however, that he was doomed to disappointment, for a thorough search of the shrubbery in and around the spot revealed nothing.

Returning to the brink of the cliff he took the pre-caution to call out before showing himself.

"José."

"*Que gente?*"

"I am Leslie. Do not shoot."

"Very well, *señor.*"

Looking over the cliff, Leslie saw that his effigy had been decapitated, even as he had expected. It was well, too, that he had had the forethought to call out, as José had dismounted and was standing behind his pony, his carbine pointing across the saddle.

"Did you see it, José?" he asked.

"No, *señor,* but I heard it. Praise God it struck as you expected."

"So I see," replied Leslie, regarding the headless effigy, "but unfortunately I wasn't on the job to strike as I expected. I may as well ride back to camp now and think up a new scheme. This one won't work again. I'll keep to the cliff above you in case of another attack."

"Very well, *señor.*"

9

BACK at camp, Leslie's men greeted him with a flood of questions, for they had heard the sound of his carbine. The appearance of José leading the horse which bore the headless effigy increased the amazement of the Mexicans, and Leslie left the task of explaining to the guide while he sat down on his cot to smoke a cigarette and think out the situation. Hearing laughter from. the men outside as José told of the ruse, he decided that the salutary effect on them had been worth the effort, even though he had not suceeded in his purpose.

His cigarette finished, he ground it into the dirt with his heel and paced back and forth in the tent. As he was preoccupied with his efforts to think out a new plan of campaign, it was some time before he noticed that it was growing lighter outside. He stepped out, and found that most of the men had rolled themselves in their blankets to rest after the night's vigil. Two stood guard, however, and José squatted beside a smoldering fire, heating a pot of chocolate.

He was about to join the latter beside the fire when he noticed smoke issuing from the stovepipe that protruded from the side of the Anciano's hut. Evidently the hermit was an early riser. Perhaps, thought Leslie, he could offer a suggestion for the next move in the campaign. At any rate, he should be told about the boards and the effigy.

Going to the hut, Leslie rapped smartly on the door. There was no response. He rapped again. Still no response. Puzzled, he swung it open and entered. Seeing no one, he walked into the kitchen. There was nobody in sight, and no sign of a fire in the stove. Yet he had, just a moment before, seen smoke issuing from the stovepipe.

Confronted with this paradoxical situation, he stepped forward and felt the pipe. It was quite warm—almost hot. He looked out the small window and saw that smoke was billowing from the pipe even more thickly than before. This led him to make an examination of the stove. One end, he now noticed, abutted against the adobe wall at the rear of the hut. He raised a lid, and a cloud of smoke whirled up into his face. Reaching inside the stove, he explored with his hand, and found that it was coming through a pipe which connected the end of the stove with the adobe wall.

If this told him anything, it was that someone had built a fire on the other side of the wall. But how had he got there? The hillside had been partly dug away when the hut was built. Evidently the digging had been deeper than appeared on the surface. He made a quick examination of the rear wall. All appeared to be solid adobe with the exception of a row of shelves containing canned goods, cooking-utensils, and other things, which occupied one side. These were of wood, apparently built against the adobe, yet they were his only hope. He pulled on the side nearest him, but it was apparently quite firm. Pushing brought the same result. Then he tried pulling the other side, and his heart gave a sudden jump as it gave and swung toward him. The

　　　　　　　　　　　　　　　　Otis Adelbert Kline

shelving, he now saw, was nailed to a heavy oaken door with concealed hinges, the front of which was plastered with adobe.

A dark passageway yawned before him. He drew a revolver, stepped in, and pulled the door shut after him.

Pausing for a moment to accustom his eyes to the semi-darkness, he noticed that what light there was came to him from around a curve in the passageway. It was of reddish hue, and flickered weirdly in the gloom. As he advanced he noticed that the floor slanted abruptly downward.

He rounded the curve in the passageway, his moccasined feet making no sound, then came to a sudden halt; for not ten feet ahead was a sight that made his flesh creep—a grinning human skull, hovering with no apparent support, in midair. The fleshless features seemed to quiver with some ghoulish emotion, the eyeless sockets to sparkle with malignant intensity.

Conquering his repugnance, Leslie again advanced, and discovered that the skull was hung on a thin, black, hence invisible, wire just at the entrance of a square room. The apparent motion of the bony features was caused by the flickering light of a fire that crackled in a fireplace cut into one wall, and over which a huge black cauldron bubbled.

Stepping past the skull, Leslie was confronted by a charnel array that rivaled, if it did not exactly resemble, the most ghastly corners of the Catacombs. He was surrounded by skulls, some dangling from the ceiling rafters on wires of various lengths, some grinning down at him from the wall where they were arranged in divers geometric patterns, and the rest piled in a grim funebral pyramid in the center of the floor.

Feeling sure there was someone near by, Leslie looked carefully about him. There were two entrances to the chamber, the one by which he had come, and another in the opposite side of the room. After investigating the second opening, which led into a dark runway, he walked to the fireplace, curious to know what was being cooked in the kettle.

Peering over, he saw a seething mass of liquid with a dark spot in the center. Then the dark spot moved — it was black hair — and the ghastly dead face of Pedro, turning with the movement of the water, looked up at him. Beneath it, another head was slowly turning toward him — the head of Miguel. He drew back, sickened and horrified, then paused, listening intently. Distinctly, he heard the sound of footsteps in the passageway he had not yet explored.

With catlike quickness, he bounded noiselessly into the passageway by which he had come, and trusting to the comparative darkness for concealment he waited a few feet from the opening.

Prepared as he was for strange sights, Leslie

　　　　　　　　　　　　　　Otis Adelbert Kline

gasped in amazement at the weird figure that entered — a tall, gaunt being, attired from head to foot in tight-fitting scarlet, and wearing a Mephistophelian hood and mask. As the man advanced to the center of the room with the springy tread of an athlete, Leslie saw that he was well muscled, and would make no mean antagonist in a rough-and-tumble fight. In his right hand he held a coiled rope, one end of which extended over his shoulder. He turned and eased a burden to the floor — a queer-looking contrivance that was fastened to the other end of the rope. It was cubical in shape, each dimension being about twelve inches, and was apparently made of steel. Projecting from the bottom on each of two opposite sides were three stout bars about four inches in length. Between each middle bar and corresponding end bar was stretched a powerful steel spring. The rope was fastened to an iron ring riveted near the bottom.

The demoniac figure knelt on the floor beside the thing and fondled it as one might a faithful dog. Then there issued from behind the hideous mask a horrid peal of laughter that caused cold chills to run up and down the spine of the American, for it was the same sound he had twice heard before, and each time after a headless victim had been found on the road.

The maniac — for such he appeared to be — continued to stroke the thing that lay on the floor before him.

"You have done well, *degollador mio*," he said. "Heh, heh, heh, my little one, you have done famously. Never was there a headsman like you. I swear it. Three heads between two suns! *Cáspita!* If the harvest continues thus, our vow will soon be fulfilled. Had that cursed Gringo not evaded us with his clever tricks we should have had four, but never mind my pretty. I promise that you shall taste his cursed heretic blood ere another sun has set. Heh, heh, heh! We will fool this self-styled 'Devil-Fighter,' my little one. We will send him to try conclusions with Sátanas and his imps. But we must rest ere that is done, so now to business."

So saying, he half raised one end of the contrivance and pressed his knee against it. Then he grasped the two middle projecting bars and pulled them toward him with some difficulty because of the resistance of the powerful springs. At the sound of a sharp click, he released his hold and the bars remained where he had left them, the springs now drawn taut the entire length of the sides. He took hold of the ring, and gave the whole thing a shake. A gory head rolled out upon the floor, and Leslie instantly recognized the face of another of his guards, probably caught napping in the early morning hours.

Seizing it by the hair, the maniac carried it to the kettle and dropped it into the boiling water. Then,

Otis Adelbert Kline

drawing a heavy machete from his sash, he prodded within the kettle, apparently testing the tenderness of the others.

Leslie, feeling that the time for action was at hand, stepped softly into the room, his six-shooter ready for action. The killer stood with his back toward him, still prodding the grisly contents of the kettle, but, loathsome and deserving of death though he was, Leslie could not shoot him down in cold blood.

"Surrender or die," he shouted.

The maniac swung around, and with the same movement, hurled the heavy machete straight for the breast of the American.

10

LESLIE had no time to dodge the keen blade of the killer that was hurtling toward his heart.. He could not possibly have moved his body fast enough. He could move his hands, however, with lightninglike rapidity, or he would never have lived to earn the title of "Two-Gun Bart." With a movement quicker than eye could follow, he parried the blade with the barrel of his six-shooter, then covered his enemy once more as the weapon clattered to the floor.

"Your last chance, *hombre*," he roared, bounding forward. "Do you surrender?"

"I yield, *señor*. You see I am unarmed. What would you?"

"First remove that mask, that I may see what servant of Satan hides behind his features."

"But, *señor*—"

"Remove it, I say!" He jammed his gun into the midriff of the killer.

"Let me go. I will pay you well—make you rich. The government offered you twenty thousand pesos. I will double it. I will—"

"Dog!" With a sweep of his free hand Leslie tore the mask away. As he did so, a long, tangled beard tumbled down over the scarlet breast and the little watery eyes of the Anciano looked into his! Then the straight back bent, the shoulders assumed a familiar droop, and the voice became a sibilant whine.

"Mercy, good *señor*, *en el nombre de Dios!* Would you slay a helpless old man?"

"A cold-blooded murderer deserves no pity."

"But I was justified. I swear it. Give me a chance to explain."

"You couldn't possibly be justified, but if you are anxious to talk I'll listen for a little while."

"*Gracias, señor*. Do you know who and what I really am?"

"I know you as Tio Luis, the Anciano, and recently, as Tio Luis, the murderer. Anything else could matter but little."

"Of that you shall judge. My name is not Luis at

all, but Tomas Perez. Neither am I of common mestizo stock, as you no doubt suppose. Through no fault of my own there flows in my veins enough Spanish blood to lighten the color of my skin and give me this beard, yet my people were Yaquis, and I am one of them, heart and soul.

"No doubt you have heard or read the sad history of my people. If you have not, then picture a tribe, a nation, peace-loving, hard-working tillers of the soil, oppressed for hundreds of years by every form of outrageous tyranny known to man, yet bearing it all with meekness, striving to overcome evil with good. Such was the nation of the Yaquis.

"Not content with squeezing the last peso from my people by unjust taxation, the government presently began the confiscation of our lands. A few of our sturdier souls rebelled and were promptly massacred. Then came the order for wholesale deportation. My thrifty father had acquired a small but fertile farm in the rich Sonora Valley. With the help of my mother, brother, sister and self, he had been able to eke out a meager existence and meet the extortionate demands of the tax collectors. One day the *Rurales* came with orders for the confiscation of our farm, and our deportation. We had done nothing wrong, yet we were Yaquis. That was enough for the government.

"A dashing young lieutenant was in command. My sister was pretty, and after he had ordered his men to drive us down the road like sheep, he bade her remain. I never saw her after that. With thousands of others of our race, we were transported to Yucatan, and there sold as slaves, mostly to the owners of the sisal hemp plantations. My mother died on the way — of grief, I think. My father succumbed, soon after our arrival, to the combination of hard work, cruel treatment and little food. Having the endurance of youth, my brother and I were able to keep body and soul together, though life was a constant horror. My chief consolation was derived from the good Padre who came to visit us, and who took quite an interest in me. It was in my talks with and observance of him that I gained a knowledge of priestly ways which has stood me in good stead since that time.

"But to go on. Although I have always been unusually quick-tempered, my brother had this trait to a more marked degree than I. Many times I have seen him fly into a frenzy over a mere trifle. Small wonder then, that he should, one day, let his hatred overmaster his judgment when the overseer struck him with a whip. He seized it and lashed his tormentor across the face, but his triumph was short — his end bloody — for the overseer decapitated him with his machete.

"For me this was the last straw. My sister had undoubtedly been ravished and murdered, my mother had died of grief, my father from cruelty, and now my little brother, the only one left for me to love, had been slain. All this I charged, and still charge, to the rapacity of the Mexican government.

"I was ordered to bury the body of my brother where it lay, unshriven, and mourned only by me. Over his grave, with tears streaming down my cheeks, I took a solemn oath that if ever I should be able to escape from that place alive I would take a thousand Mexican heads to pay the debt. I bided my time, and one day my opportunity came. When I left, I took with me the head of the overseer who had slain my brother.

"My first act on the open road was to rob a traveler of his mule, his pack, and his head. The pack, I found, contained a large store of cheap but gaudy jewelry which I hawked to advantage in the villages through which I passed. Whenever I saw the chance I would take a head, remove the flesh by boiling, and store the skull in my pack.

"Within a month my jewelry had all been sold and my money was exhausted. I obtained employment in the shop of a horseshoer, and it was while there that I conceived and secretly manufactured my little *degollador*, as I call it. It is so designed that when it drops over a man's head, the impact with his shoulders releases the razor-sharp blade, usually severing his head from his body. If the blade strikes a vertebra and sticks, then a sharp pull on the rope completes the job. But to go on with the story.

"I chanced to come here, and found that the place was admirably suited to my purpose. I did not live in the hut at first, but camped on the hillside not far from here. I succeeding in collecting many skulls from travelers riding beneath the cliffs, and of course I left no traces. One day while wandering on the hillside I came upon an opening that excited my curiosity. Seeing that it penetrated quite deeply I made a number of torches with dried grass and explored it. It led me to a small chamber behind the image of St. Anthony, and I found, to my amazement, that the slab which formed the rear panel of the shrine was, in reality, a door, easily opened from the inside, and swinging on brass hinges which, though corroded, were still serviceable. The drop of blood which you found at the base of the shrine bears me out in this, as I used that door when obtaining Pedro's head while you and José waited at the table for your chicken and tortillas.

"Exploring further, I found this room and its connection with the rear of the hut. The two rooms and the tunnels had evidently been used at some forgotten time by the keepers of the shrine, as a place of refuge during Indian attacks.

"That evening I took the head of Father Salvador while he was exploring the hillside for herbs. The next day, when a company of pilgrims came — they had already grown fearful of the neighborhood and came in numbers—I told them I had discovered the body near my camp. They swore he had been murdered by the devil, such being the popular superstition regarding the other deaths because I never left tracks, and it was not difficult for me to persuade them and the authorities who came later that I would be a suitable guardian for the shrine.

"One day I noticed the advertisement of a costumer in a paper from Mexico City which had been wrapped around a bottle of tequila given me by a pilgrim. I took a train down there and purchased three costumes from him like the one I now wear, giving, of course, a false name and address. The costume fitted well with the popular superstition regarding the place, and I felt that it would afford me considerable protection in case I was seen. Is there anything else that puzzles you?"

Leslie considered a moment.

"Yes. There are several things. For one, how does it happen that you can throw that thing with such uncanny accuracy?"

"In the same way that a vaquero can throw a riata with equal accuracy. By practise. I practised for weeks before I attempted to use it at all as a substitute for the machete. You are one of the very few live targets I have ever missed." He took a skull from the pyramid and handed it to Leslie. "Here. Roll this across the floor as swiftly as you wish, and let me show you."

Leslie waited for him to pick up the instrument of death and poise it aloft. Then he rolled the skull at the opposite wall. The Anciano hurled the thing with catlike quickness, but it fell, not over the skull, but over the head of the American. With a cackle of diabolical glee, the hermit jerked the rope taut.

11

LESLIE had holstered his revolver when he rolled the skull, hence both his hands were free. As the infernal machine descended over his head he instinctively put up both hands to throw it off, but this was prevented by the Anciano's jerking the rope taut. The keen blade was beneath his chin, almost touching his throat, but the trigger bars had not yet touched his shoulders. Had they done so his death would have been instaneous. Still tugging at the rope, the hermit quickly shortened the distance between them. Then, grasping the ring with one hand, he dropped the rope and suddenly pressed down on the machine from the top with the other. The trigger bars struck Leslie's shoulders, but quick as the hermit had been, the American was again a shade quicker. Shifting his own hold, he had grasped the two bars that moved the blade, using the pressure on the back of his neck to keep it from his throat. The springs were tremendously powerful and he had all he could do to keep the keen blade away, the Anciano meanwhile keeping the thing pressed down on his head and jerking at the ring behind.

The struggle that ensued was the most fearful in Leslie's experience. The Anciano, he found, was a powerful athlete, notwithstanding his previous pretended feebleness. Twice his chin was cut to the bone by the razor-edged blade as the hermit jerked him about. The thing that galled him the most was the fact that he could not fight back. Although his six-shooters were belted about him he dared not let go with either hand to reach for a gun. His sole consolation was that his enemy was in like case so far as his hands were concerned, though a long way from being in such desperate peril.

Struggling intensely, bleeding profusely from the two cuts in his chin, Leslie soon found his strength ebbing at an alarming rate. He lashed out blindly with his feet and sometimes succeeded in kicking the enemy's shins, but the softness of the moccasins rendered this ineffective.

Knowing that the unequal struggle could not last much longer, Leslie at length resolved on a desperate plan. First relaxing, to make it appear that his strength was gone, he suddenly bent double and, at the same time, pushed upward with both hands. The hermit, taken completely by surprise, was first jerked forward, then catapulted over the head of the American. Although the movement jerked the machine from his head, Leslie received a severe cut on his forehead. The blood trickled down in his eyes, half blinding him, so that he could but dimly see the hermit lying on his back where he had fallen. Whipping out his knife, Leslie cut a piece from the riata and pounced on his prostrate foe, who appeared partly stunned from his fall. It was but the work of a moment to turn him over and bind his hands behind him. Another piece, cut from the same riata, served to secure his feet.

"There, damn you!" he snarled, rising unsteadily and wiping the blood from his eyes. "I guess you won't try any more tricks."

The hermit made no answer, but there came a sound that instantly put Leslie on his guard—the clatter of boots and the jingle of spurs in the passageway through which the Anciano had come. Instantly supicious, Leslie drew both six-shooters and crouched behind the pyramid of skulls, convinced that no one but an enemy could have come from that direction. He lowered both guns with a nervous laugh a moment later, as José stepped through the doorway. Behind him came a dapper caballero whom Leslie instantly recognized.

"Hernandez!" he cried in surprize. "How the devil did you get here?"

"Ees ver' simple, *amigo*," Hernandez replied, warmly shaking the proffered hand. "I get desperate an' use the hot iron on that damn' *peón* today.

Otis Adelbert Kline

Then he's talk plenty. Ees tal me Tio Luis gave heem the order to get your head, promising heem many blessing een return. He's tal heem that he who cuts a heretic gets eight years' absolution.

"Right away, I smell the mouse, and ride out here weeth two men. José, I find cooking breakfast, an' he's tal me you're in the hut. I go there, but find no one, so return to José. He's say maybe you 'ave gone to look for the trail where you shoot at the devil last night. We go there and find trail ourselves. It leads to a hole in the hillside an' a passageway which we follow to this place. I see you 'ave those devil, all right, but where ees the Anciano? You must get heem also to win those twenty thousand pesos, for both are guilty."

"Fair enough," replied Leslie. "I call you. Take a look at this man's face."

Hernandez bent and turned the Anciano on his back, then straightened up with a cry of amazement.

"Tio Luis! Son of wan gun! You win, *amigo.*"

The further adventure of Bart Leslie in "The Cyclops of Xoatl" can be read in **TALES FROM THE PULPS #5**.

TO THE READER

If you enjoyed this book, you will be glad to know that there are many others just as well written, just as interesting, to be had in the Fiction House Press Library.

You will find the Fiction House Press Library online at

www.FictionHousePress.com

www.ingramcontent.com/pod-product-compliance
Lightning Source LLC
Chambersburg PA
CBHW030538030726
47495CB00004B/1048